SURVIVING
Middle School

SURVIVING
Middle School

An Interactive Story for Girls

Dave McGrail

Langdon Street Press | Minneapolis, MN

Langdon Street Press
322 First Avenue N, 5th floor
Minneapolis, MN 55401
612.455.2293
www.langdonstreetpress.com

ISBN-13: 978-1-63413-129-2
LCCN: 2014918489

Distributed by Itasca Books

Cover Design and Illustrations by Lauera VanDerHeart
Typeset by B. Cook

Printed in the United States of America

To my kids, my inspiration

Preface

To the kids:

In real life, you are bound to face many of the dilemmas depicted in this book. Some of them will be fleeting and possibly fun to mull over; others will be more serious. I hope you will talk them through with your friends, your school counselors, and, yes, even your parents.

To the parents of girls who are about to make the leap to middle school:

Buckle up.

It was a great summer—horseback riding camp in July, beaches with giant waves in August, and ice cream every Friday and Saturday night. Now it's back to school. You are starting sixth grade, your first year of middle school. You went shopping with your mom over the weekend for an awesome first-day-of-school outfit: a denim poof skirt, a hot pink tank top, and combat boots. You are dying to see your school friends and find out your homeroom teacher.

Fifth grade was a breeze. You got good grades and were invited to tons of birthday parties. You even landed the role of Molly in *Annie*. This year your sister, Annabelle, joins your school as a kindergartener. Other than that, sixth grade will be just like fifth grade, except better. Right?

Maybe not. On the first day of school you spy Madison and Lexi sitting together in the cafeteria. They have hated each other since first grade (when Lexi threw Madison's Hello Kitty hat out the bus window); today they're laughing like longtime BFFs. Chris Barvess, who was the third-shortest kid in your class last year, is almost as tall as your dad. Kids are clustered around a foreboding poster that reads, "Mark Your Calendars: The Sixth-Grade Dance Is September 29th!"

[Turn to page 3.]

As soon as you find a seat next to your best friend, Liza, the bell rings and an unfamiliar man shuffles into the cafeteria. He is only about five foot two inches tall, but he is stooped over so he appears even shorter. He must be eighty-five years old, and he has enormous eyebrows resembling two overfed woolly bear caterpillars. He is totally bald, which makes his eyebrows stand out even more.

Just as it crosses your mind that he should consider a trip to the barbershop for his eyebrows alone, he shouts your name in a thick German accent. You jump so suddenly that your knees hit the table. He proceeds to rattle off the names of twenty-two other sixth graders. Halfway through the list you realize that this senior citizen is your sixth-grade homeroom teacher. It turns out he's your math teacher as well.

[Go to the next page.]

Fifteen minutes later Old Eyebrows leads you to your homeroom. Everyone takes a seat. He says, "My name is Mr. Haller. I vas a code breaker and an astrophysicist for zee government for seventy years. Now I am here. I vill teach you and you vill learn." You wonder what a code breaker does. Your brain is still a bit rusty from the summer.

Seventy years! You do the math in your head—if he's eighty-five now and he worked for the government for seventy years, then he must have started at age fifteen. You lean over and whisper to Liza, "Can you believe . . ." but before you finish the sentence, Mr. Haller bellows, "Young lady! Vat is your name?" You tell him your name. From the crinkling of his bushy eyebrows you guess that a question is brewing, likely the standard first-day-of-school question, some version of "What did you do over the summer?"

[Go to the next page.]

But Mr. Haller does not ask you about your summer. Instead, he asks you, "If two trains, seekz hundred miles apart, are heading toward each other on zee same track, vith vun train traveling at fifty miles per hour, and zee other vun traveling at seekzty miles per hour, ven vill zey SMASH into each other?" He yells the word "SMASH" and simultaneously pounds his fist on the table, and once again you jump so high that your knees hit the desk. If your knees could speak, they would most certainly ask you, "Hey, what's your problem?"

And that's when it finally sinks in. Dorothy is not in Kansas anymore. It's a whole new ballgame, and the old rules don't apply. You are no longer in the fifth grade. This is middle school. Forget about thriving; this year will be about merely *surviving*. Are you up to the challenge? Will you make the right decisions? Let's find out. . . .

[Turn to page 7.]

With your brain frozen on images of mass casualties from the approaching train wreck, Mr. Haller loses patience, sighs loudly, and moves on to the next student, Lexi Nexus, who, like every other student in the class, is now sitting straight up in her chair, eyes wide with terror.

Mr. Haller spends the next forty-five minutes barking a math question at each student, jotting down responses on a notepad and, it appears, assigning seats depending on the responses.

"Zeez vill be your seats from September first through June tventy-second," he says, and then he asks Lokesh Chowdhury how many days there are between September 1st and June 22nd. (Lokesh answers, "I'm not sure, Mr. Haller, but it feels like it might be a long, long time." Mr. Haller is not amused.) The first day of school has not started off well.

[Go to the next page.]

Finally, recess! You are looking forward to picking up where things left off last spring, with a game of freeze tag. But none of your classmates are running around. Instead, the boys are just standing around with other boys, and the girls are talking with other girls. There is one exception. A group of eight kids is huddled in a circle, staring at something on the ground. You make your way to them, peek over Madison's shoulder, and ask, "What's going on, guys?"

[Go to the next page.]

All eight kids turn and stare at you, and you sense that your timing is terrible. You soon find out why. On the ground is a small worm. It's very much alive, twisting violently. John McGrath speaks up. "She'll do it. She's brave." He is talking about you. He is holding a twenty-dollar bill. In the split second before you figure out what's going on, you take note of John's unruly blond hair and striking green eyes. Before now, you'd never noticed how cute he is.

[Go to the next page.]

That thought leaves your mind the second the challenge becomes clear—they are daring you to eat this squirmy worm. The reward is twenty dollars, plus your classmates' respect (especially John's).

[If you accept the challenge and guzzle the worm, turn to page 12.]
[If you refuse, go to page 14.]

You pick up the worm and hold it high above your head. It wriggles furiously, as though it knows what's coming. You close one eye, think about John and the twenty dollars, and drop it down the hatch without chewing. You can feel it sliding down your throat and making its way toward your stomach. This continues for a couple of minutes. It's a bizarre, unpleasant feeling. You start to sweat and are on the verge of vomiting when suddenly the movement stops.

"Wow, that was awesome!" says John. The others nod their heads, impressed.

You collect your twenty dollars, not sure whether it was worth it.

• • •

With the drama concluded, the girls and boys separate. The girls break into groups of three or four while the boys start a dodgeball game. You notice that Liza is talking to the most popular girl in the grade, Kim Basta.

Suddenly, John McGrath shouts at you, "Hey, wanna play dodgeball?" This is unprecedented. The girls *never* play dodgeball with the boys.

[Go to the next page.]

John is smiling, and something makes you want to play. You're really curious, however, to find out what Liza and Kim are talking about.

[If you give dodgeball a shot, go to page 18.]
[If you thank John for the invitation but jog over to Liza and Kim, go to page 23.]

You pick up the worm. It's a revolting creature, covered in a layer of slime and dirt and, below that, a layer of slimier slime and dirtier dirt. You are afraid that if you pinch it any tighter it will pop and splatter its guts all over your hand. Suddenly it hits you that you're actually considering eating this gooey, wriggly, gross thing. No thanks! You drop it on the ground.

Somebody whispers, "Wimp," but no one appears all that interested in taking up the challenge. John is already off playing dodgeball. You're not sure if you'll ever have another such opportunity to impress him (or the other kids), but it was just too disgusting. At dinner that night, you barely touch your plate of spaghetti.

[Go to the next page.]

The next school day is a busy one. Mr. Haller gives you a writing assignment—for homeroom. That's not even a class! Liza gets the Industrial Revolution as her topic and groans a bit too loudly. You get Abraham Lincoln and the Gettysburg Address. You are delighted; your dad is a huge Civil War buff, and for as long as you can remember he has been telling you stories about Honest Abe. Mr. Haller has required each student to type at least four double-spaced pages. You are genuinely interested in the topic and actually start your research that night.

Three days later, you are typing with uncharacteristic speed. Before you know it, you have two pages completed. On your way to the kitchen for a snack break, you somehow manage to collide with the wall. That's right, you literally hit the wall. Uninjured, you are amazed at your own clumsiness. Sometimes you crack yourself up.

[Go to the next page.]

It's not quite as funny when you return to your computer and figuratively hit the wall, unable to say anything else about Abraham Lincoln or the Gettysburg Address. Why couldn't the Gettysburg Address have been longer so you'd have more to write about? Your dad stops by and launches into a fifteen-minute lecture on your topic. Somehow even this doesn't provide you any new material for your paper. It's no use—you could stare at the computer screen for four score and seven years and you wouldn't be able to come up with another word. And the paper is due tomorrow!

[Go to the next page.]

As you are struggling mightily to make it to page three, you click on a link and stumble across an article about Abraham Lincoln and the Gettysburg Address, written specifically for kids. The author is a historian, David Donald, and he seems to know a thing or two about Abraham Lincoln. As you scroll over the article, you realize you could easily copy and paste a large section of it into your paper and it would fit perfectly. If you do, your paper will probably end up being at least four pages. Of course, you'd change around some of the words. . . .

[If you don't use the article, turn to page 26.]
[If you do use the article, turn to page 32.]

The last time you played dodgeball was when you had a substitute teacher for gym class about two years ago. You remember it being a lot of fun, and you recall having a conversation with Liza while in the middle of the dodgeball circle. It was about unicorns.

You are soon reminded that the object of dodgeball is to *dodge* a *ball* when one whizzes by you at what seems like a hundred miles an hour. Holy cow, when did the boys start throwing the ball so hard? About thirty seconds into the game, Chris Barvess hits you in the head with a ball and you crumble to the ground. You get back up, take your place outside the circle, and do your best to hit John with a ball, in part because you blame him for roping you into dodgeball and in part because it's kind of fun targeting him.

[Turn to page 20.]

The bell rings, recess is over, and you head back inside. One new thing about sixth grade is the lockers. Mr. Haller hands out locks to each student. He gives you and your classmates five minutes to memorize your combinations and then orders everyone to tear up the pieces of paper with those combinations, mumbling something about codes being more important than you can ever imagine.

Kim Basta spends the entire five minutes putting on lip gloss with a pocket mirror. Although Kim has been nothing but mean to you since the first day of kindergarten, you have to admit that she is really pretty, even more so with her sparkly pink lips. Your parents would never let you wear makeup to school (even lip gloss), and you are more than a bit jealous of Kim. Anyway, as you slip into the bathroom, you see Kim standing in front of her locker, staring blankly at the lock in her hand. You smirk as you think, *Next time spend a little less time on your beautiful lips, Kim, and you'll remember your combination.*

[Go to the next page.]

When you emerge from the bathroom, the hallway is empty. Kim's locker is the only one without a lock. The custodian, Mr. Dubois, is whistling a Bruce Springsteen song in the boys' bathroom, some distance away. He has left an enormous garbage bin in the hall, directly under Kim's locker. A quick glance inside the gray plastic bin reveals the regurgitated contents of Brian Jake's breakfast. Gross.

A word about Kim Basta. In kindergarten, she teased you relentlessly about your Abby Cadabby lunchbox until you switched to brown paper bags. In first grade, she "accidentally" stepped on your diorama of the rain forest. In second grade, she stuck the sticker from her apple on your back twenty-one days in a row. In third grade, she started the deeply distressing lice rumor. In fourth grade, she invited every girl in the class to her birthday party—except you. In fifth grade, she pointed to you when the school librarian asked for volunteers to help restack books during recess. (And you were chosen.)

[Go to the next page.]

No one is looking. You open Kim's locker and peek in. There is a small, laminated picture of some boy band taped to the door, along with a collage of her "besties." (Yes, the collage is actually labeled "BESTIES.") She must have been thinking about how to decorate her locker all summer.

The contents of her locker include an expensive-looking purse, the book *Twilight*, and a gigantic pink makeup bag. Of course, you would never steal, but what if her stuff were to find its way into the garbage bin situated so invitingly below?

[If you quickly and quietly dump the contents of Kim's locker into the garbage bin, go to page 29.]
[If you don't dump Kim's stuff into the garbage bin, go to page 35.]

You decline John's invitation and head toward Liza and Kim. Having learned your lesson (from the worm incident) about the dangers of opening your mouth too quickly, you casually listen while they talk.

Then Liza suddenly pulls you into the discussion. "Guess what?!" she says. "I'm going to ask Chris Barvess to the dance!" She has a huge grin on her face. You look at Kim. Kim is also smiling, but it's not a genuine smile. You smell a rat.

Chris Barvess has hated Liza since the second grade, when she started calling him "Chris Barf Face" after he threw up on the monkey bars. Although he fought the nickname for a year, it stuck and he eventually gave up. But he has not forgotten how it originated. In fact, this morning, before the bell rang, when Matt Thurber said, "Hey, Barf Face, how was your summer?" you saw Chris look at Liza like he wanted to strangle her.

[Go to the next page.]

You know that Kim knows exactly how Chris feels about Liza. On the one hand, you want to tell Liza not to ask Chris to the dance, because she will only be humiliated when he rejects her. On the other hand, if you tell her this, *you* will hurt her feelings, and she may be angry at you.

[Go to the next page.]

It's not an easy decision, but you'd better make up your mind because Liza is heading in Chris's direction. You're still not sure what to do, but if you don't get to Liza quickly, the decision will be made for you. You start running to her as fast as you can. You feel like the famous sprinter Usain Bolt, except for a key difference: he probably hasn't ever tripped over a heart-patterned backpack and fallen flat on his face. You do. Miraculously, no one sees your epic fall. You get up and dust yourself off, relieved not to be hurt. But Liza is only a few feet from Chris and you are still at the other end of the courtyard.

Suddenly Chris turns around and begins running in the other direction, away from Liza. You figure that he has seen her coming and is trying to avoid the encounter. But, upon closer inspection, you spot an abandoned dodgeball at the edge of the courtyard and realize that Chris is just retrieving it. He hasn't even noticed Liza, who is now waiting by the door for him, nervously chewing her hair. There is still time!

[If you tell her not to ask Chris to the dance, go to page 40.]
[If you decide to stay out of it, go to page 41.]

You are tempted, but you don't use the article. Instead, you squeeze out another half a page in which you note that Gettysburg, Pennsylvania, is located near Route 30 and experiences its heaviest rainfall in June. You know it's not a good ending, but you call it quits anyway. When you hand in your paper the next day, it crosses your mind that perhaps you could have incorporated the Lincoln article by quoting some portions and summarizing others completely in your own words.

You glance at the essays your classmates are handing in, wondering if anyone else dared to write fewer than four pages, and that's when you notice Davina Clark's homework planner and get absorbed in a different thought entirely: John McGrath.

[Go to the next page.]

Davina has "I ❤ JM" scrawled all over her homework planner, her locker, and her arms. She spends most recesses talking about John's hair, his eyes, and his cute smile. While you couldn't agree more, you remember fondly a time not so long ago when recess was simply about jumping rope. Davina clearly has changed since you two first became friends four years ago. Still, notwithstanding her infatuation with John, you know Davina is a good kid with a good ❤ .

Davina's JMO—her John McGrath Obsession—is in full swing today, and you half-listen as she leans over to you and begins describing his perfect earlobes, his shoes, and a freckle on his cheek, pledging to tattoo his middle name, which she claims to be Maximilian, on the bottom of her foot the day she turns eighteen. She stops talking for a moment when Mr. Haller says, "Now review your homework planners." Then she whispers something that catches your attention. "So promise me that you won't go out with John this year. I know you won't, but I just want to make sure."

[Go to the next page.]

Whoa. It's one thing to let her blabber on about John. It's quite another to make such a promise, especially when you think you might have a huge crush on him as well.

[If you tell her that you can't make that promise, turn to page 45.]

[If you do make the promise, turn to page 47.]

Sweet, sweet revenge. The contents of Kim's locker fall with a soft *thud* into the garbage bin. You peer down. Her stuff has settled right into Brian Jake's former breakfast. You whisper to yourself, "Good-bye, glittery pink lips."

The gleeful feeling of vengeance lasts exactly twenty seconds, and then you wonder how much trouble Kim will be in. Will her parents find out that she's lost all of her makeup? Cosmetics aren't cheap. Will they yell at her? Will she ever find out how *Twilight* ends—whether Bella picks Edward or Jacob?

You lean over to see if you might at least rescue the makeup bag. If you didn't smell the garbage before, you smell it now. It stinks. You can't find the makeup bag. It must have fallen to the very bottom. You stand on your tiptoes, lean over the rim of the giant garbage bin, and reach deeper, gingerly moving the contents of the garbage bin around. You spot something pink and lean over a bit more, stretching every muscle in your body to reach it.

[Go to the next page.]

You lean too far! You teeter on the edge, a human seesaw, and then fall in. Right into the puddle of vomit. Can this get any worse?

[Turn to page 52.]

You include a portion from the historian's article. With the help of an online thesaurus, you simplify some of the more complex words. You show it to your dad, who says he is impressed and proud of you. Somehow you forget to mention the article to him. You agree that your paper is brilliant, so you title it, "My Brilliant Paper About Abraham Lincoln and the Gettysburg Address."

The next morning you wake up beaming, arrive to class beaming, and turn in your paper, still beaming. When Mr. Haller collects your paper, he flips through the pages for about thirty seconds and says, "Zis looks very goot."

Then he explains plagiarism to the entire class. He describes plagiarism as using another author's language, thoughts, ideas, or expressions as though they are your own. This lecture is probably triggered by Justin Clocknee's paper about the Boston Tea Party, which he "wrote" by simply copying the "Tea Party" Wikipedia page. (And as it turns out, the Boston Tea Party and the Tea Party are quite different.)

[Go to the next page.]

But then the thought crosses your mind that perhaps your paper, the last one Mr. Haller looked at, prompted the plagiarism lecture. Now you're concerned that you shouldn't have included those excerpts from the historian's article in your essay, even though you did change a lot of the words. You're not sure, but if you could do it all over again, you might choose differently. Did you plagiarize?

You mull this over until recess, when you find yourself faced with another dilemma. While ducking behind a tree during a game of freeze tag, you look down at your feet and, lo and behold, there is a fifty-dollar bill staring back at you.

You snatch it up and put it in your pocket. "Finders, keepers," you murmur gleefully. Now you finally have enough money to buy your sister the birthday gift she's been asking for nonstop for the past two months—a chinchilla. Perhaps you'll surprise her and your parents! And yet something is gnawing at you (and it's not a chinchilla).

[Go to the next page.]

You say to yourself again, "Finders, keepers," but with less enthusiasm, as you start to consider the rest of the expression ("Losers, weepers") . . . and the situation. Hmm. It makes plenty of sense when you are searching for shells or sea glass on the beach. Is finding money any different?

[If you keep the money, turn to page 48.]
[If you take the money to the principal's office, turn to page 50.]

You decide not to get revenge on Kim Basta, at least not in this way. You close her locker and back away. Good thing, too, because at that moment Mr. Dubois emerges from the boys' bathroom, still whistling Springsteen. He sees you and gives you a half-wave. You would have been caught red-handed. As you stroll back into the classroom, Kim actually compliments your hair, and now you're really glad you didn't trash all of her stuff.

• • •

Your classes go smoothly, although who decided that dissecting a frog in science class should happen right before lunch? At the end of the day, you see a bulletin board notice that says, "Sign Up Your Parent to Chaperone the Dance." You know that your dad would love to chaperone. He has always volunteered in the past, even though the field trips and events have taken place during work hours, which you know is not always easy for him. He has even signed up for trips that were not all that exciting, like your first-grade visit to the paper clip factory. (The only bright spot was when Lokesh Chowdhury insulted the tour guide by asking if he could borrow a stapler.)

[Go to the next page.]

You love your dad's sense of humor . . . most of the time. He is completely goofy, but sometimes he's a bit too goofy. Last year, he declared one Saturday "National Yoda Day." It was pretty funny, but you were mortified when Rachel Webster came over to work on a school project and your dad croaked at her, "Peas for dinner you would like?" Rachel just stared at him. Meanwhile, your little sister, Annabelle, responded, "Peas I want not, but have carrots I will. Herh herh herh."

[Turn to page 51.]

It's a Thursday morning, and you can hardly keep your eyes open. Mr. Haller drones on and on. At recess you find a shady tree, lean against it, and look up at the clouds. One looks like a plunger. Weird.

A soccer ball whooshes by, followed by Brooke Nelson giving chase. She stops to ask why you aren't playing. You tell her you're exhausted. Brooke is on your gymnastics team, and you can't understand why she isn't as tired as you. She looks over her shoulder, kneels down, reaches into her pocket, and pulls out three tablets the size of baby aspirin.

You have flashbacks to the scene in *James and the Giant Peach* where the old man gives James the crystals. . . .

"Don't look so freaked out," Brooke says. "They're not drugs or anything. They're just caffeine pills. My mom buys them for me at the drugstore. It's no big deal. They help me stay awake. Go ahead, you can have them."

[Turn to page 39.]

The warning not to do drugs has been drilled into your head for as long as you can remember, but you've always trusted Brooke, and she's telling you that these pills aren't drugs. (In fact, you know that caffeine is a basic ingredient in coffee.) If her mother gives them to her, they must be safe. And you would love to have the energy to play soccer with your classmates. But still . . .

[If you politely decline the pills, turn to page 82.]

[If you try them, turn to page 84.]

You get to Liza just in the nick of time. As Chris walks toward her, you position yourself between them. He gives you a confused look, steps around both of you, and makes his way back to class.

"What are you doing!?" Liza asks you. "I was just about to ask him to the dance."

"I know," you respond. "I was stopping you. Liza . . . he doesn't like you. He would have said no. Kim was setting a trap for you."

Liza lets your comment sink in. She reacts just as you feared she would. "You have no clue!" she yells. She storms off.

She never asks Chris to the dance. You think this means she realizes you were right, but if that's the case she doesn't show it. Instead, she remains angry at you for the rest of the week. The next week you start acting like friends again, though your relationship feels a little strained.

[Turn to page 55.]

You freeze in your tracks. Maybe it's not your place to butt in. You watch everything unfold from a distance, reminding yourself that sometimes in life you expect the worst and everything turns out okay. This is not one of those times. It's like watching a terrible accident in slow motion.

You see Liza mouth some words to Chris, smiling and staring at him, then looking at the ground, then at him, then at the ground. When Liza is done talking, Chris is motionless for about ten seconds, at which point he bursts into laughter. He is laughing so hard that his face turns a reddish-purple and he clutches his side. You hear him exclaim, "My friends won't believe this!" and he runs off.

Liza begins sobbing quietly. You run to her and give her a hug. When she realizes that you saw the whole thing, she begins blubbering uncontrollably. For the rest of the week, she is visibly sad and extremely quiet, but after the weekend she is back to her old self, talking about anything and everything that crosses her mind, mostly pottery and puppetry and a new craft she has invented, "potterpuppetry."

[Go to the next page.]

The bell rings, and you're on your way to art class with the diminutive Ms. Solomon. Ms. Solomon resembles a hobbit in stature and in dress, and on more than one occasion you've wanted to check to see if her feet are tufted with hair. Unfortunately, she is not a sandal-wearer, so there's no way to know for sure.

You love the fact that Ms. Solomon is always positive, complimenting your artwork whenever possible, even though you know you are no Van Gogh. "Beautiful apple tree!" she once said about your sea turtle sculpture. Your painting of the circus was a "fantastic sunset." "Love the still life," she remarked about your self-portrait (and you're hardly pear-shaped). Her enthusiasm never fails to give you a boost, no matter how disconnected from reality it might be.

So art class is usually a serene place. But not today. As you lean over to put the finishing touches on your papier-mâché birthday cake (a.k.a. "cute hat"), you notice that your pants have what appears to be a small paint stain on the inside of them. You touch the stain and stare at your finger in confusion, followed by shock. Followed by horror. There is blood on your finger.

[Go to the next page.]

Your period! You don't know how you know; you just do. You look down, thankful that you changed out of your white shorts and into light brown jeans before leaving for school. The room suddenly seems to be spinning. Crystal McGregor is looking at you. Does she know?! What should you do? If you leave now, it will be obvious there's something wrong, but what choice do you have?

Ms. Solomon interrupts your thought process. "Class," she says, "I see that most of the boys have finished, but period girls were talking and have not done so." What?! Period girls? Or was that "myriad girls"? What's a myriad?

Although you're panicking inside, you try to act casual as you slip your sweatshirt over your head and tie it around your waist. Avoiding eye contact with anyone, you walk out of the room and head to the bathroom. Now what? You know you've discussed your first period with your mom, but now that it's actually happening, you're completely drawing a blank.

[Go to the next page.]

You struggle to remember your mom's advice, but all you can think of is that hilarious *Camp Gyno* video on YouTube. You've heard that if you fold up toilet paper and stuff it in your underwear, it will stop the blood from spreading. The only other option is to go to the school nurse, although you're not really sure what she will be able to do for you, and you might be too embarrassed to explain what's happening.

[If you head to the nurse's office, turn to page 57.]
[If you try the toilet paper trick, turn to page 62.]

You think it through and politely respond, "I'm sorry, Davina. I'm afraid I can't do that."

It is not the answer she was expecting. She is completely floored and, for once, speechless. At that moment the bell rings, saving you from further awkward silence. You feel a little bit guilty, but you never know what the year will bring and you don't want to make promises you can't keep.

Later that day you learn that Davina has asked five other girls the same question and they have all agreed not to go out with John. You are the only one who refused. By the end of the day, everyone knows about your refusal. This is not the attention you want. You are in the process of second-guessing your decision . . . when it happens.

[Go to the next page.]

"Hey," John says to you while you wait for the bus.

You are mesmerized by his piercing green eyes, and it takes a few seconds before you get your head out of the clouds.

"Hi," you respond, unable to come up with anything more interesting.

"I'm pretty sure that I saw Ms. Solomon's feet today and they are covered with hair."

You know just what he means. You've always thought that Ms. Solomon, your unusually stubby art teacher, might actually be a hobbit. Maybe John McGrath is not only cute but also totally on your wavelength.

"No way!" you respond. You're still searching for that interesting, witty comment.

"Yeah, but even if she's a hobbit, she's pretty nice," John says. He doesn't seem to notice that you're standing there agog without much to say. He adds, "She told me that she really liked my clay cup even though it was obviously a bald eagle."

[Turn to page 64.]

Figuring that your friendship with Davina is more important, you raise your right hand in an oath-taking gesture and promise not to go out with John McGrath during sixth grade. Maybe he'll have a crush on you next year.

No sooner do you make this promise than Davina is out of sight and John McGrath himself approaches!

"Oh, man, please tell me that you didn't also promise her?" he says.

He sees that you are confused.

"Davina is making all of her friends promise not to go out with me. It's so stupid. And, well, I was kind of hoping . . . you'd like to do something on Friday."

He says this with pain in his voice, as though he fears he is too late.

Oh, no! Oh, tragedy! . . . Or not. What should you do?

[If you tell John that you just made a promise and you can't break it, turn to page 65.]
[If you break your promise to Davina and agree to go out with John, turn to page 67.]

You keep the money but decide not to buy a chinchilla for your sister, lest you get stuck cleaning its cage. That weekend, while at the mall with your family, you mention to your dad that you're going to duck into Claire's Accessories to buy some jewelry with your own money. You tell your dad, not your mom, because your dad basically turns into a zombie at any mall, staring ahead with empty eyes and repeating the phrases, "Okay, I'll be right here" and "What is this country coming to?"

True to form, your dad responds, "Okay, I'll be right here." You head off to Claire's and spend $49.35 on ten bracelets, a tie-dyed headband, three lip glosses, and some neon nail polish. This is a true shopping spree!

[Go to the next page.]

On Monday, you are passing by Principal Knivner's office and you overhear the school custodian, Mr. Dubois, say, "What can you do? I was going to use that money for my granddaughter's birthday gift." There is a pause, and then you hear Mr. Dubois utter, "Absolutely not. I can't take your money. That's very generous of you, but it's not the end of the world. I'll figure something out." He walks out of the office and gives you a friendly smile.

You ask, "Everything okay, Mr. Dubois?" He says, "Yeah, darling. I lost fifty bucks last week in the courtyard and was hoping it would turn up. No such luck."

You feel terrible. The new bracelet and headband you are wearing suddenly feel like they weigh one ton each. If you could go back in time, you would have brought the fifty bucks to Principal Knivner. Mr. Dubois would have claimed it and been able to buy a birthday gift for his granddaughter. And if he didn't, maybe Principal Knivner would have simply given you the money for your honesty. Lesson learned . . . the hard way.

THE END

You turn in the money to Principal Knivner. He thanks you, compliments you on your honesty, and tells you to come back in a week; if no one claims the money by then, it's yours, he says. For about an hour, you can't stop thinking about the money, but eventually you forget about it altogether.

A few days later, the custodian, Mr. Dubois, finds you in the hallway. "You know that money you returned last week? That was my bonus from another job. It had fallen out of my pocket. Principal Knivner told me you turned it in, and I want to thank you. I was able to buy a birthday gift for my granddaughter, and I got something for you, too." He hands you a box. Inside is a surprisingly stylish bracelet from Claire's Accessories. You are touched. He clearly had thought about what a sixth grader like you might like and then made a trip to the mall to get the jewelry. You wear the bracelet for the rest of the year.

THE END

Incidentally, your dad loves to dance. But his dance style is a bit unorthodox. He shuffles around the dance floor for a few seconds and then suddenly, as though he has just been struck by lightning, he jumps up and all of his body parts shoot in all directions at once. Then he shuffles again. Then lightning strikes. Shuffle, lightning. Shuffle, lightning.

The school dance will be held on a Saturday night, so it wouldn't conflict with your dad's work. But there's a good chance that he'll do something that will completely embarrass you, like dance.

[If you sign him up to chaperone, go to page 68.]
[If you figure he won't know what he's missing and choose not to sign him up, go to page 78.]

It turns out that it can get much worse. Mr. Dubois is standing over you. "What's going on here, darlin'?" he asks. You think up a lie and you think it up quick. You tell him that you were fiddling with your earring while walking by the garbage bin and that it slipped out of your earlobe and fell in. Mr. Dubois asks why you don't have an earring in the other ear. You tell him that the newest thing is to pierce only one ear. He asks you why neither of your ears is pierced. You want to tell him that you've been begging your parents to let you pierce them, but you realize that answer is just a bit off topic.

You can feel your face turning red. Suddenly the garbage bin feels like an oven. Are you actually sweating or is that just your imagination? Mr. Dubois looks at the locker, peers into the garbage bin, looks at you, looks inside the garbage bin again, sifts around a bit, and finally says, "Darlin', I was born in 1948. Was that yesterday?" You shake your head. "Darn right it wasn't."

Can this get any worse?

[Go to the next page.]

It turns out that it can get much worse. You've got to stop asking that question. Mr. Dubois wheels his garbage bin—with you in it—to the principal's office.

Principal Knivner was a police officer for twenty-five years before becoming head of your school. He is a gigantic man with large jowls and a neck almost as thick as his head. He speaks quietly, but somehow this only adds to the intimidation students feel when called into his office. He asks what you and the contents of Kim Basta's locker are doing in the garbage bin.

It's no use lying to Principal Knivner. He is renowned for his ability to spot a lie a mile away, and you have heard that kids who lie to him are treated more harshly than those who come clean. So you tell him the truth, starting with the Abby Cadabby lunchbox you had in kindergarten. When you get to the lice rumor, you start to cry and you don't stop for the remaining twenty minutes of your story. There, you've told the truth, with tears to boot. The worst must be over.

[Go to the next page.]

Wrong again. Principal Knivner, who has listened patiently to your entire story, leans across his desk and says, "Thank you for your honesty. If you'd lied you'd have been suspended for three days. But two wrongs still don't make a right, and this is a serious offense, almost as bad as stealing. I am suspending you for the rest of the day. Call your parents. Someone needs to pick you up." Sixth grade just gets worse from that point on.

THE END

Sixth grade is exhausting. On top of the social drama, you have homework and other commitments, including gymnastics practice twenty hours a week. Your team is contending for a state championship this year, and you, an accomplished trampolinist, are a major reason for that success.

Your coach, Nicolae Ceaușescu, Jr., is fond of saying that "weakness is just a state of mind." His other favorite expressions are: "Never show weakness," "Weakness must not break you and it must not bend you, for you will lose points," and "Newborn kittens are weak; you are not a newborn kitten!" The man does not like weakness. Practice is grueling, and by the end of each three-hour session, you always want to curl up in a ball and go to sleep. But you can't because when you get home there is still a shower to take, dinner to devour, and homework to complete.

Over the past month, you have fallen asleep in the following places: the breakfast table, the shower, standing in line for movie tickets and during the movie itself, and, yes, on the toilet.

You wish that, with a snap of your fingers, you could magically energize yourself whenever you are tired.

[Turn to page 37.]

You grab a couple of donut holes and call it a day. Most of your classmates try a wide variety of foods, and there are murmurs of delight and surprise at how good they taste. The plantains, in particular, are gobbled up in no time.

You immediately regret not trying some new foods, especially since Intercultural Day ends in sixth grade. You mention this to your dad when you get home from school, and he promises to try to do a better job of exposing you to new foods. Then he serves you microwaved mac 'n' cheese for dinner.

• • •

Ten years later, as you finally start trying new foods, you ask yourself, "Why didn't I know about this before?" You think back to the missed opportunity that was your sixth-grade intercultural celebration.

THE END

Inspired by the straight-talking girl from the *Camp Gyno* video, you get your courage up and march to the nurse's office. The nurse, Ms. Flotsam, is a kind, grandmotherly woman. She is sitting in a chair when you arrive, as though she has been waiting for you. There is no one else around, and her office is a silent oasis in the midst of the hustle-bustle that is your school.

She takes one look at the expression on your face and the sweatshirt tied around your waist; then, with the understanding air of someone who's seen this a hundred times before, she reaches into her desk drawer and pulls out some leggings, a clean pair of underwear, and a rectangular, pink, plastic package like the one your mom showed you when she told you about pads. She finally speaks: "It's okay, sweetie. We've all been there." She explains how to use the pad and directs you to the bathroom adjacent to her office. You leave with a feeling of comfort and protection and—after Ms. Flotsam says, "Congratulations"—maybe just a little bit of pride.

[Turn to page 59.]

It's been an exhausting day. You head to library skills class. Even though you've already had lunch, you're suddenly starving. You reach into your bag and pull out . . . a chocolate chip muffin, your favorite treat. Score! Typically you would have finished this during lunch, but today you spent too much time trying to touch your tongue to your nose (you are so, so close) and didn't get to the muffin.

You are about to take a bite when you see Rachel Webster racing toward you, yelling, "Stop!" She reaches you in time to say, totally out of breath, "Don't eat that."

"Why not?" you ask. Given the effort she has made to stop you, you expect her to tell you that the muffin is laced with poison.

Instead, she responds, "That thing has about a thousand calories. You'll have to do like four hours of gymnastics to make up for it."

[Turn to page 61.]

Rachel explains to you that she is the leader of the Diet Club, which includes Laticia Smith and Lexi. The purpose of the club, she explains, is to be healthy and to avoid eating any junk food. She asks if you want to join. The idea is appealing. Your parents are always telling you that it's important to have a balanced diet, and you like Rachel and Laticia (and are okay with Lexi).

[If you join the Diet Club, turn to page 86.]
[If you don't join, turn to page 88.]

Unable to bear the thought of anyone, including the school nurse, knowing about your first period right now, you try the toilet paper trick as a temporary solution and head back to class.

It fails. Actually, this qualifies as an epic fail, as the bloodstain on your pants slowly grows larger over the course of the next few hours. You keep going back to the bathroom to replace the toilet paper, but the rest of the day at school is completely nerve-wracking. You can't cover your pants with your sweatshirt forever. As the afternoon buses arrive, you breathe a sigh of relief, believing you've escaped unnoticed.

Then, to your horror, Lokesh Chowdhury yells, "Hey, you've got something all over your pants!"

Think fast! Think fast! "Yeah. Ha. I'm sooo clumsy. I spilled ketchup on my chair at lunch and then sat in it." *Lokesh*, you think with intense concentration, *I'm not the person you are looking for. Move along, Lokesh.* Thankfully, Lokesh just shrugs his shoulders and goes about his business.

[Go to the next page.]

This has been the most stressful day of your life. When you get home, you tell your mom everything, with more than a few tears. She listens intently. When you get to the toilet paper trick, she asks (not in a mean way) if you remember the talk the two of you had about your period being completely natural and nothing to be ashamed of. She asks why you didn't go to the school nurse and get a pad, as you had discussed.

She says that at least you'll have a good cautionary tale for your girls when you are a mom. That doesn't make you feel much better.

THE END

There is a long pause, during which John stares at the ground.

Then, in a weird voice that you've never heard from him before, he pops the question (while still looking at the ground): "So, do you want to hang out sometime?"

It's so sweet how shy he is. Your heart is beating a mile a minute and you are burning up, but in a good way.

You've never been asked to "hang out" before and, frankly, you're not entirely sure what this means. Would you be boyfriend-and-girlfriend, or would you actually go somewhere? (The movies? The hardware store?) Or both?

[If you say, "Sure, okay," turn to page 91.]
[If you ask him exactly what he means by "hanging out," turn to page 106.]

It is not easy, but you tell John you just can't go out with him.

Sometimes things move very quickly in the sixth grade: by the end of the day Davina and John are going out. Whatever that really means. There is only one other sixth-grade couple, and much of the courtyard conversation over the next few weeks involves Davina and John. They are always together, in the halls, in the cafeteria, in the auditorium. It's as though they are magnets, attracting each other at all times.

And then suddenly, inexplicably, they cannot be seen within a hundred feet of each other. Someone must have changed their magnetic poles, you think. (You are studying magnets in science class.) They are no longer a couple.

A month later you find yourself waiting with John McGrath for the bus. You chat about your favorite TV shows, about Mr. Haller, and about Mad Madeline's Ice Cream Parlor, which you agree has the best ice cream on the planet.

[Go to the next page.]

There's a comfortable pause in the conversation, and the thought of asking him out crosses your mind. After all, he said two months ago that he had a crush on you. Then again, aren't the boys supposed to ask out the girls? And would you be breaking your promise to Davina?

[If you ask him out, turn to page 92.]

[If you just get on the bus, turn to page 93.]

You tell John that you'll go out with him, and together you make plans to head to Mad Madeline's Ice Cream Parlor that Friday after school, with his older sister, Lydia, joining you. You are super excited . . . for about five minutes; that's when Davina finds out.

"I can't believe you broke your promise in about thirty seconds," she says. She is really hurt. You don't know what to say. You almost wish she'd do something bad, like spread a false rumor about you, but she doesn't. Although you eventually start talking again, your friendship is never the same. The guilt you feel is almost too much to bear.

Your relationship with John McGrath lasts exactly eight days and ends when he almost breaks your nose in dodgeball. (It was an accident, he claims, but was it really necessary to throw the ball that hard four feet away from you?)

Sixth grade is basically a bust.

THE END

You add your dad's name to the list of parent chaperones and tell him later that evening. He is ecstatic. On the day of the dance, he dresses up in a three-piece suit and dons a polka-dotted bow tie. You can't figure out whether he looks chic or ridiculous. Probably a little bit of both. The dance, which is held in the school gym, is surprisingly fantastic. The DJ takes requests from the kids. You ask him to play your favorite song. It is such a hit that two other kids request the same song! You and your friends spend almost the entire time dancing together.

The boys sit on the bleachers and punch each other in the arm. A couple of brave ones meander onto the dance floor, but for the most part they just stand there looking uncomfortable. Your dad, on the other hand, can hardly contain himself; he twitches from time to time, and you are sure that he wants nothing more than to dance with you and your friends, especially when the kids run out of requests and the DJ starts playing '80s music. This makes you anxious, and you wonder whether inviting him to chaperone was a good idea.

[Go to the next page.]

But then the DJ announces that, during the last fifteen minutes of the dance, he will be playing a few slow songs to help wind things down. This announcement takes both the boys and the girls by surprise, and there is absolute panic as all the kids try to find dance partners. There are about twice as many girls as boys, and the frenzy to pair up is like an evil version of musical chairs.

Even worse, when the first slow song starts, you are getting a drink at the water fountain in the far corner of the gym. By the time you realize what is going on and make your way back to the dance floor, just about every boy is standing close to a girl, trying to figure out how and where to hold onto her. You spot Justin Clocknee, a small brown-haired boy known primarily for his never-ending supply of gummy bears. Seconds later, Rachel Webster is holding his hand, heading toward the dance floor and visibly breathing a sigh of relief. A number of girls are dancing in pairs. You are the only kid without a partner.

[Turn to page 71.]

You feel yourself starting to sweat when suddenly someone literally sweeps you off your feet and brings you to the center of the dance floor. It's your dad. He starts swaying back and forth with you and smiling, while trying to remove a speck of dust from his eye. You shrug your shoulders and give your friends a "What can I do?" look. They smile back at you. It's mildly embarrassing, but sitting on the bleachers while everyone else dances with a partner might have been even worse.

• • •

The following week at school, you expect some teasing from Kim Basta, but it doesn't happen. Something is different about her this year, and it's not just that she looks like she should be in high school. She's been kind of nice to you. There was that one day when your parents forgot to pack your lunch and she gave you her carrots. And on another day, she scribbled "Love ya" on your notebook after you caught her peeking at your math homework answers. She even complimented your poof skirt, describing it as "retro."

[Go to the next page.]

It's a dreary Tuesday afternoon, and with only a few more minutes left at recess, your best friend Liza's asthma acts up and she has to go to the nurse's office. Not the worst thing in the world since she had been talking on and on about her favorite topic, pottery, for the past five minutes. You kick around a rock, waiting for the bell to ring. Then you hear your name called. "Come hang out with us!" says a voice from across the courtyard. It is Kim Basta herself! She is with four other really popular girls. You mosey across the courtyard and say, "Hi." It's not hard to pick up the threads of conversation—lip gloss, who has a crush on whom, favorite songs, cool earrings at Claire's Accessories.

This is unprecedented. Everyone has pretty much formed their cliques by sixth grade, and it's a big deal when someone leaves or enters a clique, especially when it's the most popular girls' clique. You can sense that other kids are looking at you and whispering.

[Go to the next page.]

You can't understand why you've suddenly gone from "normal" to "super popular," but why look a gift horse in the mouth? (For that matter, why look any horse in the mouth? Who wants to get a big whiff of horse breath?) The bell rings, and you head inside with Kim and your new group. You are laughing hysterically, for no particular reason.

As you enter the classroom, Kim turns to you and says with a big lip-glossy grin, "We needed some new blood. The six of us will have so much fun together!"

"Sounds great," you say, and you mean it. Everyone looks at you differently for the rest of the day. You have an extra little bounce in your step.

[Go to the next page.]

The meaning of "the six of us" becomes apparent the next day. At recess, Brooke Nelson is chasing down a soccer ball and comes within ten feet of your new group of friends. Your friends glare at Brooke. She is not welcome a step closer. Brooke gets the message, lets the ball go, and retreats. When Lokesh Chowdhury approaches your group and asks for change for a dollar, no one even responds to him. It's as though there is a force field around your group, which other kids try to penetrate at their own risk.

[Go to the next page.]

And then it hits you. Liza. No sooner do you think about her than she is walking toward your group, a puppy-dog smile on her face. Now would be a good time for your dormant powers of mental telepathy to awaken. *Turn around, Liza,* you think. It's no use. She is waving to you, babbling something pottery-related, somehow entirely oblivious to the predicament she is about to put you in. Kim Basta whispers in your ear, "Tell her you're busy. You'll see her in class."

[Go to the next page.]

There's no escaping. The rest of your sixth-grade experience and beyond could be shaped by the decision you need to make right now.

[If you tell Liza that you're busy and you'll see her later, go to page 94.]
[If you simply walk away from the popular girls and greet Liza, turn to page 95.]

The thought of your dad attending the dance is too much to bear, so you decide not to sign him up to chaperone. Word travels fast among parents, however, and when you get home that night he says, "I hear there was chaperone sign-up today." Your sheepish expression is all it takes for him to infer the whole story. You can sense he's a little hurt, but then he mentions that he never let his parents come to his basketball games. By the end of the night he seems fine and trounces you in poker. Your dad is cool in his own way.

The dance, which is held in the school gym, is surprisingly fantastic. The DJ takes requests from the kids. You ask him to play your favorite song. It is such a hit that two other kids request the same song! You and your friends spend almost the entire time dancing together.

But a couple things dampen the mood. Rachel Webster's dad is one of the chaperones. He sits on the bleachers and looks at his phone the whole time. This really annoys you, but you can't explain why. With a twinge of guilt, you imagine your dad fighting the urge to break out his shuffle-lightning moves.

[Go to the next page.]

The dance has other lingering effects. You are wearing a white dress that is kind of plain but still cute. When you enter the girls' bathroom at some point around the middle of the dance, Kim Basta is on her way out. She looks you up and down, and you brace yourself for an insult about your dress or hair. But she manages to cut much deeper. "I'm afraid I'll have to alert the Department of Forestry about your legs," she chirps as she passes you.

You look down at your legs. They are, indeed, pretty hairy, at least compared to other girls' legs. But no one has ever said anything about them before. You know that this comment from Kim is just the beginning— and you have to give her credit, it's a clever insult, especially for her. That night you come up with a pretty good response about alerting the Department of Education about Kim, but by then the opportunity for a comeback has long since passed.

[Go to the next page.]

Back at home, you confront your mom and ask her whether you can shave your legs. You've had this discussion before. And, just as before, she says "it is inappropriate" for a sixth grader to be shaving. In your experience, when your parents forbid you from doing something because it is "inappropriate," that's just their way of saying they can't give you a good answer (and don't have to). Your mom is firm. Under no circumstances are you allowed to shave your legs until seventh grade. You tell her that you'll just wear pants all year. This is a bluff; you love your skirt supply too much, and there's nothing worse than trying to run in jeans in 85-degree weather. Your mom calls your bluff, responding, "That's fine with me. It's almost winter anyway." Thanks a lot, Mom.

[Go to the next page.]

The next day at gymnastics practice, you encounter a group of five girls in the locker room, all crowded around Emily Murray, another sixth grader. Emily is a nice girl and quite popular at the moment, for she is holding an electric razor. The girls are shaving their legs. Brooke Nelson has just finished hers. Emily offers you the razor and says, "It might not be a bad idea for you."

Emily has never said a mean word to you or anyone else, and you feel like she has your best interests in mind as she passes you the razor. You really are hairy. You know that your mom will be unhappy if you do it, but she's never given you a good reason why you shouldn't, and this might be one of those rare instances when it makes sense not to do *everything* your parents tell you. Besides, when will you have this opportunity again?

[If you take the razor and shave away,
go to page 99.]
[If you decline Emily's offer, go to page 103.]

You can't quite put your finger on why you tell Brooke, "No, thanks," but you do. That evening you decide to tell your mom about what happened. She's deeply absorbed in *Inkheart*, which she claims she is reading to make sure that it's appropriate for kids your age. (You know better—she still loves young adult fantasy books.) When you bring up the subject of the caffeine pills, your mom puts the book down and a rare serious expression comes across her face.

She explains that caffeine is, in fact, a stimulant drug even though you can buy caffeine pills in a drugstore. She says that if a sixth grader were to go to Starbucks and order a Venti cup of coffee, she would hope the Starbucks employee would ask for confirmation from an adult before taking the kid's money. She says, "Make no mistake about it, caffeine is addictive, and it is not appropriate or healthy for any sixth grader to be taking caffeine pills. Among other things, people who regularly consume caffeine actually get headaches when their bodies start craving it."

[Go to the next page.]

Your mom is scaring you a bit, though you can tell she's proud of you for making the right choice and not taking the pills. She encourages you to come to her before making any other tough decisions in the future.

Then she asks who offered you the caffeine pills. You say that you'd rather not tell her and that it doesn't matter anyway since the girl's mom buys them for her. Your mom insists that you tell her. You know that, if you do, she'll call Brooke's mom. You don't want to get Brooke in trouble, but you realize that if your mom is right—if sixth graders shouldn't be taking caffeine pills (and you now believe she is right)—maybe you should tell her, because you don't want Brooke to keep doing something that could be harmful to her health.

[If you reveal Brooke's name, turn to page 107.]
[If you refuse to reveal Brooke's name,
turn to page 109.]

You swallow the tiny tablets. At first you don't feel anything, but after about ten minutes, it hits you. You feel like a Disney character who has suddenly regained the strength previously sucked out of her by a conniving villain. You go bounding across the courtyard and join the soccer game. (It is not particularly organized to begin with, so no one notices that your entrance into the game makes the teams uneven.) You are WIDE AWAKE during class, at dinner, and at gymnastics practice.

As you get into bed, you are sure that you made the right decision—those tiny little caffeine pills turned you into a ball of energy for a few hours, and it was great! You close your eyes, pleased with yourself. Then your eyes spring open. You can't sleep. Your mind is racing and you can feel your heart pounding. After about a half an hour of staring at the ceiling, you dig your trusty stuffed animal (a giraffe appropriately named Trusty) out of the closet, sure that she will help you get to sleep.

[Go to the next page.]

No luck. You count sheep. You count the frustrated beeps of the living room smoke alarm in need of a battery change. You count backwards from a thousand . . . and you get to zero! The last thing you remember before you finally fall asleep is glancing at the alarm clock—3:15 a.m.

You wake up the next day a zombie. You thought you knew sleep deprivation before, but it was nothing compared to this. You are so tired that you start crying in your cereal. When your mom asks you what's wrong, you tell her you had a bad night's sleep. You don't say anything about the caffeine pills, which you have figured out were the cause of your sleeplessness.

At recess, you are back under the same tree, but this time you are actually asleep when Brooke Nelson wakes you up . . . and offers you more caffeine pills. You now know that it's a bad idea to take them, but you are so, so tired. Oh, boy, what have you gotten yourself into?

THE END

"Sure," you say. You join the Diet Club. You force yourself to toss your muffin in the trash. You are still starving, however, so you suggest to Rachel that the two of you ask Liza if she'll share a couple of fruit bars from the endless supply she keeps in her bag. "Nope," Rachel says, "those aren't allowed either."

It turns out that it's easier to make a list of the foods you *are* allowed to eat as a member of the Diet Club than those you are *not* allowed to eat. Most of the foods on the "Allowed" list are pretty bland: carrots, saltines, rice cakes, and the like.

The next day you and the rest of the Diet Club are huddled together, and Lexi mentions that she has lost three pounds since she joined the club a couple of weeks ago. Rachel and Laticia congratulate her, so you join in and congratulate her, too.

[Go to the next page.]

Laticia asks how much weight you've lost. You tell her that you have no idea; you just joined the club yesterday, and you thought it was all about healthy eating. The other girls urge you to hop on the scale as soon as you get home so that you can track your weight loss.

That night you drag the scale out from under your parents' bed and check your weight.

[Turn to page 116.]

You opt for your favorite dessert over Rachel's proposal. Chocolate Chip Muffin 1, Diet Club 0. Being healthy is a good idea, but it's not the same as dieting, and when you ask Rachel which foods are on the restricted list, she simply responds, "You'll know them when you see them." The whole idea seems fishy (though it's not clear whether fish is on the restricted list). Besides, you are already a member of the Trending Boy Band Fan Club, the Floss at Recess Club, the I Spy Club, and G.A.S.P. (Girls Against Strict Parents).

You kind of regret not learning more about health issues now, but perhaps Rachel Webster is not the most qualified instructor. There is a mandatory Health Issues class in seventh grade; you figure you'll be fine waiting until next year to get the facts straight on dieting.

[Go to the next page.]

The next morning at the breakfast table, your parents discuss who will pick you up from early dismissal. As is often the case on early dismissal days, parental pickup duties are decided by heated debate at around 6:30 a.m. Today's negotiations conclude; it has been decided that your dad will pick you up and, in exchange, your mom will get the dry cleaning, set up dental appointments, and buy fruit for the week at the farmer's market.

When school gets out at noon, you and your dad travel back home on the subway. It's been a long week, so he lets you play games on his phone. Apparently you're not the only ones for whom it has been a long week. Directly across from you, lying upon a row of subway seats, is a street performer who seems to be snoozing. You can't be totally sure he is asleep because he is wearing a gigantic Elmo head, with the rest of his costume in a bag near his feet. In addition to the red furry mask, he's wearing a T-shirt that says, "I'm With Stupid." It is a hilarious sight, and you are having a tough time containing your laughter. Your dad shoots you a look; he, too, is trying to hold back a smile.

[Go to the next page.]

You wish your friends could see this. You get an idea and point to the camera button on your dad's phone. No longer smiling, your dad pauses to consider the request, then raises his eyebrows and tilts his head as if to say, "It's your decision."

Suddenly you're not so sure whether you want to take the picture. Is the guy awake? Will he see you and get offended? Even if he does see you, maybe it's worth it. It will be *so* funny. And your dad isn't objecting to the idea.

[If you don't take the picture, turn to page 111.]
[If you do take the picture and send it to your friends, turn to page 114.]

"Sure, okay!" you say, maybe a bit too enthusiastically.

"Great!" John says and darts onto his bus.

Phew. You breathe a sigh of relief. That was nerve-wracking. And awesome.

The rest of the day is like a dream. You feel light-headed as you replay the conversation in your mind over and over, pretty much from the moment you step onto the bus until the moment you fall asleep.

At school the next day, you are still floating on air, but now you have to figure out exactly what it means to be "hanging out" with someone.

You and John stand next to each other at recess, barely speaking. Meanwhile, a number of kids giggle and point at you, as though you are zoo animals. You feel simultaneously embarrassed and proud.

[Turn to page 122.]

You have no idea how you find the courage, but you blurt out, "Do you wanna hang out with me sometime?"

John's face lights up. "Sure, yeah, great," he says. At that moment, both of your buses arrive and you go your separate ways.

The birds are singing, the sun is shining, and you are walking on air.

Your first relationship, with John McGrath, lasts the entire year and it goes great.

On the last day of school, John tells you that his mother just took a job in Walla Walla, Washington, and he will be moving in two weeks. You both cry your eyes out and then laugh at the name Walla Walla until you cry some more. And then, for the first time, you kiss.

THE END

You and John go your separate ways and you immediately regret not having asked him out. Who says a girl can't ask out a boy? You are upset with yourself and resolve to ask him out the next time you get the chance. But the chance never comes again, at least not in the same way it did when the two of you were waiting for the bus.

You don't want to talk about it with your parents or friends, so a few weeks later you tell your five-year-old sister, Annabelle, about the whole thing while she is coloring. You figure she must be only half-listening, but when you finish talking, she stops what she's doing, looks you in the eyes, and says with uncanny clarity, "You gotta strike while the iron is hot." Then she continues her search for the green crayon. Where does she pick this stuff up anyway?

THE END

You say, "Liza, I'll catch up with you in class, okay?" You say it so nicely that you're certain Liza's feelings won't be hurt. But Liza is no dummy. She stops and stares at you. Then she turns around and walks away. Kim draws you back into the conversation about whether glitter is cool or childish. The girls are divided on the issue; they're having a heated debate. You half-heartedly participate, already trying to figure out how to mend things with Liza.

Liza sits alone at lunch. You know that you have hurt her feelings, but you don't really have a plan to make things better. Besides, you promised Kim and Cassie that you'd make rubber-band bracelets with them at lunch. Maybe tomorrow will be better.

[Turn to page 124.]

You walk toward Liza without looking back. It's hard enough hearing the snickers of Kim and the popular girls; seeing the expressions on their faces would be unbearable. You ask Liza to tell you more about the largest kiln she has ever seen, and her face lights up. To your relief, a couple of minutes later she says, "You know what? I'm kind of sick of talking about pottery." You spend the rest of recess jumping rope and making up ridiculous knock-knock jokes. By the time the bell rings you aren't even thinking about the popular girls, a.k.a. your former "friends." You wonder how it could have been so difficult to decide between Liza and them. You know you made the right choice, and you and Liza have a blast all the way back to class, cracking each other up with images of Mr. Haller waterskiing in a Speedo.

[Go to the next page.]

Though you wouldn't exactly say that you like Mr. Haller, you eventually get used to his quirky ways, including his almost religious devotion to the honor code. All of his students have signed a pledge that they will not lie, cheat, or steal.

Mr. Haller is also all about "building character." He often reminds the class, "Encountering and beating temptation builds character." But he has some weird ways of applying this virtue. When you really have to pee, building character means holding it in until Mr. Haller is done with a lesson; when it's ten degrees below freezing, building character means braving the cold in order to get "fresh air" during recess; and, for some reason, building character also means sharpening pencils with a handheld pencil sharpener instead of the electric version. You begin to wonder whether there's really any difference between "building character" and being miserable.

Every Tuesday and Thursday, you have Mandarin Chinese class with Ms. Chang. Ms. Chang is the polar opposite of Mr. Haller: she is young, tall, beautiful, and chic. Sometimes Mr. Haller sits in on Ms. Chang's class. He says he is interested in learning Mandarin.

[Turn to page 98.]

One particular Thursday you are in an especially silly mood. Ms. Chang is working with the students on their brushstrokes as they strive to replicate the Mandarin characters on the blackboard. She draws the character for "baby" on the blackboard. It looks a little bit like two robots. You pull out the books from your backpack and, leaning them this way and that, create a 3-D version of the character for "baby." You start giggling uncontrollably. "Hey, Mr. Haller!" you shout from across the room. "Look, I'm building character!" Mr. Haller looks up from the notes he is taking and simply nods. Other kids turn around and look at you like you've lost your mind. But you persist.

"See, Mr. Haller? Character—I'm building character." You are laughing hysterically at your joke. He tells you to "simmer down and pay attention." Literally falling out of your chair, you repeat, "Building character! Building character!"

"Zat's it, young lady. You're vith me at recess!" Mr. Haller declares.

[Turn to page 127.]

You take the razor and shave until your legs are as smooth as a baby's butt. They feel great. You leave the locker room with a spring in your step. You pass Kim Basta, of all people, on the way out. She looks at your newly shaven legs and blurts out something to the effect that you're still "hairy at heart," but you both know that her insult doesn't have quite the same force this time around.

That night you wait for your mom to notice your legs and give you a hard time, but she is completely oblivious. It takes three days before she even mentions it, at breakfast, while you are still half-asleep.

"I thought I told you no shaving your legs until seventh grade," she says sternly. "I am disappointed that you blatantly disobeyed me."

You feel bad but, interestingly, she does not punish you. And, man, your legs are smooth!

A week later, you reflect upon your decision and conclude that you made the right one. Two months later, however, when your legs are, it appears, even hairier than they were before you shaved and Emily Murray is no longer bringing her electric razor to gymnastics, you will not be so sure.

[Go to the next page.]

But, for now, you are so pleased with your newly shaven legs that you take a selfie in your neon pink tube skirt and post it on Instagram. You don't have your own phone or iPad or Facebook account, like a lot of your friends do, so you often feel that you are missing out on fun conversations. Hopefully using Instagram, which your parents have recently authorized, will change all of that. You are so excited that you call Liza and Emily Murray and let them know that you have just set up an Instagram account and posted your first picture. They call Tamika Banks, Stephanie Rose, and Valentina Lopez. In a heartbeat you have five followers, and they all comment on your first picture: "QT!" "Love it and love ya!" "OMG so cute!" "Yay u r on!"

By the end of the day, you have a dozen followers and by the end of the week thirty followers, including some you never would have expected, such as your Great Aunt Fanny, who once mistook a calculator for the remote control.

[Go to the next page.]

You wonder how you ever survived without Instagram. You even meet some new friends on Instagram—five boys your age become your followers. They are from all over the country, which is pretty cool. One of them, "Darth Creampuff," is a sixth grader from Dayton, Ohio. He posts a lot and is really funny. He has cool manga character pictures all over his Instagram page and his screen name makes you laugh every time you see it. When you post selfies in your "Happy Birthday" hat, complete with "candles" that light up when you press a button, Darth Creampuff says, "LOL . . . I'll bet you can't take a picture with shoes that are just as crazy." It turns out that you have a ridiculously funny pair of glittery red shoes that light up whenever you walk. You slip them on your feet and take a picture with the family iPad. It is absolutely hilarious. Post on Instagram? Or are you getting too carried away with this?

[If you don't post, go to page 130.]
[If you do post, go to page 134.]

With your conscience clear, you demonstrate your Balloon Vacuum to the entire school and a slew of parents at the science fair a couple of days later. Although you do not win the purple ribbon, your project generates more interest than any other one, including Michael Rosenberg's. In fact, there are more people looking at Ceara Mahoney's project, "Potato in a Box," than Michael's because they can't figure out what Ceara's is all about. (It turns out that it is literally just a potato in a box.)

Parents are exceptionally complimentary of the Balloon Vacuum. "Wow, that's a great idea," they say. "Balloon pieces left on the ground are really dangerous for toddlers." There is a long line of students who want to try it out. Teachers ask you a bunch of questions, which you are easily able to answer. You notice that Mr. Haller hovers around your project, with arms folded and a half-smile. It is a good day.

THE END

With your mom's voice echoing in your head, you walk out of the locker room. So many other girls take a turn shaving, though, that it seems you are now the only sixth-grade girl on the planet with hairy legs. And Kim Basta reminds you at least once a week that your hairiness is not going unnoticed.

Fortunately, your mom surprises you with some really cool, comfortably light pants and leggings so you can cover your legs, if you want, for most of the school year. There are definitely moments, usually involving Kim Basta, when you wish you could go back in time and take that razor from Emily, but you realize this will all be a distant memory by the summer, when your parents will finally buy you your own electric razor.

[Go to the next page.]

The shaving decision behind you, you turn to lunchroom dilemmas. When it comes to eating your lunch, every day is a new adventure, and not in a good way. Both of your parents work, so they share grocery-shopping responsibilities. You have often thought they need a personal assistant to coordinate shopping, as they sometimes both buy the same food and then your whole family has to race to eat up two dozen bananas and finish the milk before it goes bad. More often, however, neither one buys the groceries. You once opened the refrigerator, looking for a snack, and found only an onion, a hunk of Parmesan cheese, and a lonely lime. No ketchup, no pasta sauce, nothing else. It is currently one of those weeks, which does not bode well for your lunch selection.

[Go to the next page.]

Sure enough, your mom scrounged together the following for your lunch: broccoli, two waffles (no syrup), a bruised and battered apple, and a plain tortilla. Blech. Liza sits down across from you with her lunchbox, featuring a picture of a kiln and the words "Pottery Power" in gray letters. (Where did she find that?) The first thing she takes out is a colossal piece of chocolate cake in the shape of an isosceles triangle. (Mr. Haller has recently been teaching geometry.) The frosting must be an inch thick. It looks delicious.

Liza says, "Doesn't Dad know that I'm allergic to chocolate? Jeez." She offers to trade her cake for— wait for it . . . wait for it . . . your broccoli! Yes, yes, yes, yes! Before you can accept, you recall the school's "No trading food" policy. This policy has rarely, if ever, been enforced. Your parents are the bigger problem. You know they would not want you trading your vegetable for a gigantic piece of cake, especially given that you are celebrating your cousin Joey's birthday that night and there will definitely be cake. But you're pretty sure they'll never find out, and is it really that big of a deal?

[If you take the cake, go to page 136.]
[If you decline the cake, go to page 137.]

"Maybe, but exactly what do you mean?" you blurt out.

"I dunno," he says. "I just mean, do you want to go out?"

You can't help yourself: "You mean hang out at school or go somewhere?"

He wasn't prepared to be interrogated.

"Go . . . out. Not school . . . out . . . somewhere," he responds, not making any sense.

At that moment his bus arrives. It might as well be a stretch limousine; he can't get on it fast enough to escape this awkwardness.

You try to salvage something by waving to him as he leaves, but he doesn't even look out his window. The yellow bus speeds away, with John staring straight ahead, not moving, as though he's just seen a ghost.

[Turn to page 123.]

You tell your mom that Brooke Nelson offered you the caffeine pills, but you beg her not to call Brooke's mom. It has been such a crazy day that you crawl into bed with your clothes on and fall asleep. Your mom kisses you on the head, and as she leaves the room, you hear her mutter something about knowing Jennifer Nelson pretty well and being a good judge of people.

The next day Brooke approaches you. You are afraid that she's going to offer you caffeine pills again, but instead she says, "My mom found out about my caffeine pills. I guess she saw them in my book bag." She's almost in tears. "Don't tell anyone this, but my mom got me to admit that Janet Quinn was giving me the pills every day in exchange for my brownie. My mom's brownies taste like cardboard! . . . Like cardboard!" Now she is crying. "Janet's parents are going to kill her. And I have the worst headache!"

[Go to the next page.]

You feel bad for Brooke but are glad that she doesn't appear the least bit suspicious that you spilled the beans. Also, you realize now that she had been lying to you—clearly her mom wasn't buying caffeine pills for her.

You hang out with Brooke less and less as the year goes on. It is a good year overall. You get better at balancing your gymnastics and homework, catching up on sleep on the weekends. Also, you win second place in the trampoline competition at the state championship!

THE END

You refuse to spill the beans. Your mom says, "Okay," and leaves your room.

The next day Brooke again offers you caffeine pills and again you decline despite your extreme exhaustion. She rolls her eyes, shrugs, and bounces away with apparently limitless energy.

Later that week, you see Brooke trading a brownie from her lunch for a baggy of pills provided by Janet Quinn, a seventh grader with an unpleasant reputation. *So Brooke's mom wasn't buying the pills for her after all*, you realize. From then on, you keep an eye on Brooke and Janet's transactions out of sheer curiosity.

One day Brooke brings in a plastic container of brownies and gives it to Janet. Janet gives Brooke an old book bag. Hmm.

A week later there is a rumor circulating that Melissa Henvey, an eighth grader, was caught drinking beer behind a 7-Eleven and that Brooke was with her. They are in big, big trouble with everyone—their parents, the school, and possibly the Mob, though the last part of the rumor seems a bit far-fetched. Brooke quits the gymnastics team shortly thereafter. Her life is falling apart.

[Go to the next page.]

Wow, you're glad it wasn't you in Brooke's shoes. But you have to wonder, how did she end up in this predicament? Could it have been avoided? With a pang of guilt, you realize that maybe you could have helped her by telling a grown-up about the situation. . . .

THE END

You decide not to take the picture. Instead, you describe the whole scene to your friends at recess on Monday. They chuckle a bit, but you were expecting a more animated reaction. You find yourself trailing off sheepishly, "You really had to be there. . . ." At least you have an idea for the "Captured Moments" essay that is due in a couple of weeks for language arts.

• • •

That afternoon, Mr. Schoen, your language arts teacher, assigns the first chapter of a new book called *Another Book About Dragons and Stuff*, which he describes as "original and groundbreaking." He informs the class that the book is available only online as an e-book and that it costs $12.95. He gives you the website information and asks you to pass it along to your parents.

That evening, you tell your mom that you need to buy an online book for school. She says, "Okay, honey, just let me know when it's time to enter my credit card information." Then she continues to cook dinner while simultaneously talking on the phone, replacing the garbage bag, and writing a check.

[Go to the next page.]

You grab your stuffed giraffe, Trusty, go to the website, and discover that the book happens to be written by Belinda Schoen, who you guess is Mr. Schoen's wife. Why are you reading a book by your teacher's wife? That doesn't seem right. But you figure an assignment is an assignment. You go to the website and are about to click "Pay Now" when you receive an email with the subject heading, "Free Copy of Another Book About Dragons and Stuff." It's from Brooke Nelson, and it includes an attachment, which is undoubtedly the book. If you want, you can now read the assigned book for free, which only seems fair, given that it was written by your teacher's wife. You can even share it with your friends!

[Go to the next page.]

Unsure what to do, you search the Internet for "Another Book About Dragons and Stuff." Your search yields only one review, which describes the book as "quite possibly the furthest thing from original and groundbreaking." It doesn't seem right that your parents and your friends' parents should have to pay $12.95 (the cost of two giant ice-cream cones at Mad Madeline's Ice Cream Parlor). Besides, your mom is pretty busy at the moment; do you really need to bother her for her credit card?

[If you ask your mom to pay with her credit card anyway, turn to page 142.]
[If you read the free copy and email it to your friends, turn to page 144.]

You take the picture as inconspicuously as possible. If Elmo-head is awake, he either doesn't see you or doesn't care, because he doesn't budge. You text the image to five of your friends. Three of them respond almost instantaneously, telling you that it might be the funniest picture they have ever seen. You smile. It really is a great shot.

Later that day, you are checking out Liza's public Instagram page. The Elmo picture is front and center, with a comment from Liza giving you credit for taking it. You feel a little weird about this, but you get over it on Monday when it's the only thing your friends are talking about at recess.

On Monday night your dad says that he was talking to one of your friends' parents, who mentioned the Elmo picture. He asks you nicely whether you'd want people taking pictures of you on the subway, even if you were wearing a mask. You mull this over while falling asleep. You sleep poorly.

[Go to the next page.]

You are tired all week, especially by Friday, when you head to Liza's house for a sleepover. Her parents go to bed at 9:00 p.m., and you and Liza sift through their collection of DVDs. Liza holds up one called *The Shining*. That sounds like a nice, sunny title. You read the back. "It seems kind of scary," you tell Liza. "And it's rated R."

You ask Liza whether she is allowed to watch rated-R movies. You don't even know what the R stands for, but you know your parents are firm in prohibiting you and your little sister from watching movies with this rating. Liza tells you that her parents have never said she can't watch them. And she thinks it might be kind of fun to watch a movie that's a little bit scary. "We'll be together, so you won't be that scared," she argues. "Anyway, the movie was made in 1980," she adds, "before they started making the really scary movies." Also, the movie looks like it has gotten unbelievable reviews; wouldn't your parents rather you watch a classic than *Madagascar* for the umpteenth time?

She makes some very good points. She leaves it up to you.

[If you watch Madagascar for the umpteenth time, turn to page 146.]

[If you watch The Shining, turn to page 148.]

By Friday, you've been in the Diet Club for five days. At recess Rachel announces that you will each check your weight on Monday night, at the end of the three-day weekend, and report it at school on Tuesday. Sounds great—you love a good competition.

Actually, the truth is you love a good competition only when you win. Unfortunately, when you check your weight on Monday morning, you discover that it is exactly the same as it was six days ago and you realize you have no chance of winning, especially since Lexi has gotten noticeably thinner in the past week. In fact, you might be kicked out of the Diet Club.

Unsure where to go from here, you lie to your mom, saying that you aren't feeling so hot and need to skip lunch. By 1 p.m., you are so hungry that you *actually* aren't feeling so hot. You are light-headed and your stomach is grumbling in protest.

By dinner, you can't take it any longer. Of all nights for your dad to make your favorite dish! You scarf down your dinner so quickly that everyone at the table just stares at you in disbelief. But what goes down must come up. . . .

[Go to the next page.]

You spend the next hour in the bathroom throwing up. Obviously your body wasn't ready for such a rapid change. With your head on the toilet seat and your mom checking in every few minutes, you have time to reflect on the Diet Club, which suddenly seems like a crazy and even dangerous idea. You quit the Diet Club that Tuesday, before things get completely out of control.

Rachel, Laticia, and Lexi aren't happy when you quit the club, and Rachel even asks whether you think you're too good for them. You are a bit upset, and when you run into the school counselor, Ms. Martinez, at the water fountain ten minutes later, she asks you what's wrong and you tell her.

A sixth grader's fortunes are like a chameleon at a disco party—constantly changing. For some reason, by lunchtime Rachel has decided to transform the Diet Club into the Dye It Club, whose members participate in group tie-dying. You gladly rejoin the reconfigured club.

[Go to the next page.]

Luckily, Mr. Haller provides you with a distraction from the day's social drama; he sends you in search of the blackboard erasers that have mysteriously disappeared from the classroom. He says he feels paralyzed without his erasers, that it's no small responsibility, and that he has faith that you can crack the code. Ridiculous as this sounds, you know that Mr. Haller means every word of it, and you are proud that he has chosen you.

[Go to the next page.]

You confidently stride out of the classroom. Mission possible. Everyone knows that if something is missing, it can probably be found in the custodian's closet, which is downstairs near the kindergarten classrooms. When you get there, you open the door and, sure enough, three chalkboard erasers, all labeled "Haller," are wedged between a deflated basketball and a computer screen so old you bet it could fetch a pretty penny on eBay as a collector's item.

[Go to the next page.]

Smiling, you grab the erasers and head out, but then something catches your eye. There is a cartoonishly large red button protruding from the wall. Next to it is a small, faded, handwritten note taped to the wall that says either, "Do not push" or "Do not rush." Okay, it's probably "Do not push," but your parents always say that nothing in life is certain except for death, taxes, and tacos for dinner on Friday nights.

Your curiosity is killing you. The button is so bright and shiny, and everything else in the closet is so dusty and . . . chalky. It's just begging to be pushed. Besides, after your successful search for the erasers, haven't you earned the right to see what happens? You will be sure to push it slowly, in case it actually says, "Do not rush."

[If you push the button, turn to page 149.]
[If you leave the button alone, turn to page 151.]

In sixth grade, gossip spreads quicker than lice at a slumber party, and you and John have created enough gossip for your classmates to feed on for an entire afternoon.

Davina, for one, is not afraid to speak her mind. While you gather your books from your locker, she says, "How could you? You know that I've had a crush on John forever!"

You've had time to prepare for this one. "I know, and I'm sorry, but so have I. And I didn't really do anything. *He* asked *me* out."

"Well, why didn't you just tell me you liked him?" Davina asks.

"I really didn't think it was anyone's business," you respond.

Davina is quiet for a few seconds, and then she says, "Well, whatever. I hope you make me the maid of honor at your wedding. Besides, I kind of have a crush on Jimmy Gold, too."

You smile, relieved that Davina seems to have moved on to a new heartthrob.

[Turn to page 152.]

You've blown it, you think. Why couldn't you just keep your mouth shut or, better yet, simply say, "Yes"?

But all is not lost. Miraculously, John finds you in the school courtyard the next day. With almost a full day to think it through, he now says with rehearsed courage, "We should hang out sometime."

Relieved, and not about to make the same mistake twice, you respond, "That sounds great."

The tension evaporates for both of you. You even joke about yesterday's awkward conversation and come up with a brilliant plan. This coming Friday is an early dismissal day and John's older sister, Lydia, is picking him up. There is an ice-cream shop next to the school. You, John, and Lydia will go together!

Now all you need to do is run the plan by your parents. . . .

[Turn to page 153.]

Tomorrow is worse. Liza is hanging out with Crystal McGregor at recess while you chat with Kim and company. You try to approach Liza after the bell rings, but she simply turns her back to you. The same thing happens the next day. And the next. You are angry that she won't let you apologize, and you return the silent treatment the following week.

At some point during the school year, you and Liza have no choice but to talk to each other. After all, there is group work that needs to be done together for science class, and your parents are friends and always find each other at the school play and other events. But your relationship with Liza is frosty at best.

[Go to the next page.]

By the middle of the year, you and Liza have completely drifted apart, which makes you very sad. And it turns out that you don't have all that much in common with Kim and the popular girls. At some point, the luster of popularity wears off and you would gladly trade whatever social status you've gained through this clique for a friend you genuinely like. Kim is not that friend.

By the end of the year, all Kim wants to do is play a game where she picks three boys and makes you decide which one you want to marry, which one you want to kiss, and which one you want to throw off a cliff. If you don't play the game, she calls you a loser; if you do, your choices are reported to those three boys by the end of the day. The boy who has been "thrown off the cliff" never takes it well.

[Go to the next page.]

One day you tell Kim that you are sick of the game. The next day Laticia Smith and two other girls in the group see you approaching and snap, "Get lost." Your head is spinning. Can the friendships you have worked so hard to develop with these girls be over just like that? It seems so cruel.

You spend the rest of the year bouncing from one social group to another, trying to make new friends. But you can't seem to fit in with anyone. You often find yourself sitting on the concrete at recess, reading. You can't wait for sixth grade to be over.

THE END

Missing recess is not the end of the world. You sit quietly, all alone, and wonder what sixth grade is like in Brazil. The bell rings and, having served your sentence, you are looking forward to seeing your friends as they return to class. Before they do, however, the ancient Mr. Haller hobbles over to your desk, looks you squarely in the eyes, and says, "You must tell your parents zat you missed recess today, and zee reason vye. Do you understand?"

Moments after you nod your head, the implications of telling your parents start to set in. There is no doubt they will be displeased, especially given that you already had your share of "paying attention incidents" in fourth and fifth grade. You remember your mom saying that you are "out of strikes" and that next time "there will be consequences."

[Go to the next page.]

There are three extremely important events coming up. First, tonight (Friday) is movie night at home, and you are dying to see *Pitch Perfect*, which is all your friends can talk about. Second, you have been invited to Sage McIntyre's birthday party on Saturday. A limo will take you and seven other girls from Sage's house to a karaoke hot spot. Sounds fantastic! Third, your birthday is coming up and you believe that, if you play your cards right, maybe, just maybe, your parents will get you the puppy you've dreamed about for the past three years. Your slip-up today jeopardizes all of these plans and hopes.

[Go to the next page.]

It was so ridiculous of Mr. Haller to keep you inside during recess just for making a joke, even if you were the only one laughing! And who is he to require you to tell your parents? He may have the right to enforce the rules while you are at school, but he can't enforce them when you are home. When he asked whether you understood his directions, you nodded, but you never actually said the words, "Okay" or "Yes, I will tell my parents." Maybe your nod just meant, "I hear you" or "Yes, I understand (but have no intention of following your orders)." It's completely crazy that you could lose your puppy over a joke that didn't hurt anybody!

Other kids have stayed in for recess with Mr. Haller many, many times before. As far as you know, he has never actually asked whether they told their parents what had happened. When you get home, the first thing your mom says is, "How was your day?"

[If you just say, "Fine," and go to your room to read, turn to page 169.]
[If you tell her about missing recess, turn to page 171.]

Something doesn't quite feel right, and you decide not to post pictures of your shoes on Instagram. Later that week, there is a school assembly on Internet safety. A guest speaker warns the sixth graders about the dangers of social media. She explains that some people using social-media tools don't have the best intentions and that you have to be careful: you don't want strangers viewing your pictures on Instagram or responding to your questions on ask.fm. She tells you that, in 82 percent of online crimes against minors, the offender uses the victim's social-networking site to gain information about their likes and dislikes. That's a shocking and scary statistic.

The next day you drop the five boys following you on Instagram.

[Go to the next page.]

Too bad you can't delete Kim Basta from your life as easily as you can drop Instagram followers. Every day she ridicules you about something: the color of your pants, the height of your ponytail, the sound of your sneeze ("hez-chhh"), anything she can think of. But then something happens that makes your life slightly easier. That something is the arrival of Vijayalakshmi Balasybramanian. She has just moved from Mumbai, India, and joins your class midyear. She speaks with an accent, but so do the parents of many of your classmates. She's a nice girl with a fantastic jewelry collection—she never seems to wear the same bracelet twice, and she wears about ten each day! The two of you are friendly enough, though certainly not great friends.

Maybe Kim Basta feels threatened by Vijay's jewelry collection, as Kim has been known since kindergarten as the jewelry queen. Who knows? Anyway, Kim is cruel to Vijay from the second she arrives at your school. There are three insults that she continually hurls at Vijay: 1. "Hey, Vijay, how is it that you have twenty-eight letters in your name if there are only twenty-six in the alphabet?" 2. "Vijay, away! Vijay, away!" and 3. "Where did you get those bracelets, Vijay, the dump?"

[Go to the next page.]

None of these are particularly clever insults, but you recognize them as hurtful, especially when half the kids in the grade are following in Kim's footsteps. Indeed, you'd bet that Vijay endures about fifty insults a day, usually some combination of the three coined by Kim. You've also heard that some girls, including Kim, are teasing Vijay online as well. That's a lot of punishment; Vijay is never really safe socially. Of course, you do not participate in the cruelty. You know better. But you feel like someone should do something to stop it.

Vijay does a fairly impressive job of ignoring the cruel remarks. Even so, after about two months you spot her crying under the slide after the recess bell has rung. Mr. Haller is completely oblivious. Maybe you should say something to someone like the school counselor, Ms. Martinez. She's really nice, and Vijay has been taking an incredible amount of verbal abuse, even for a sixth grader.

[Go to the next page.]

On the other hand, you hate to admit it, but now that Vijay is a lightning rod for Kim's cruelty, you haven't had to worry about being ridiculed quite as much. Yesterday you even wore your favorite rainbow tights, half-expecting to be teased, and no one said a word. Also, your parents have told you many times not to be a tattletale. Maybe this is just one of those situations that will have to run its course naturally. Besides, if you tell an adult, Vijay's parents might get involved, and that could make things even worse.

[If you tell Ms. Martinez about the situation,
go to page 155.]
[If you stay out of it, go to page 160.]

You post the picture on Instagram. About fifteen seconds later, Darth Creampuff responds, "OMG, where did you get them?" You tell him the name of the nearby store where you got them. He replies that, by coincidence, in about a week he will be visiting relatives who live near you. Then he asks you whether you want to go see a movie when he's there. Whoa, that was sudden.

You tell him thanks, but you don't even know what he looks like. About ten seconds later he sends you a picture of himself at the beach. Wow, he is cute. He looks just like the famous lead singer from that trending boy band. Wait . . . you've seen that picture before. It *is* the famous lead singer from that trending boy band!

Suddenly you feel extremely uncomfortable. You tell him you know that's not him in the picture, and he writes back, "Maybe, but I look just like that. Let's meet and I'll prove it."

You tell him to leave you alone. He says that he can't because he loves you. You tell him that you are dropping him from Instagram. He responds, "You can drop me from Instagram if you want, but I know where you live, I know what you look like, and eventually I'll find you."

[Go to the next page.]

Now completely freaked out, you cancel your Instagram account on the spot. You tell your parents. They are visibly shaken and even file a police report, but there's not much more they can do at this point. For the rest of the year, although you never actually encounter Darth Creampuff, the thought that a strange man might be waiting for you after school has you on edge, and you often have nightmares about that possibility.

THE END

You devour the cake, which is outrageously delicious. "Wow," Liza says. "Have you not eaten in a week or something?"

"Basically," you respond.

During gymnastics practice, you can feel the cake sitting in the pit of your stomach. You aren't sick (yet), but you don't feel hungry either.

Cousin Joey and your aunt and uncle come over that night to celebrate Joey's third birthday. Your gymnastics practice runs late, and by the time you get home, everyone has eaten dinner. They're all waiting for you so the family can sing "Happy Birthday" and have cake.

Since Joey has a strange love of wombats, his ice-cream cake is decorated with a giant frosting wombat. Before you know what's happening, your uncle hands you an enormous piece of cake. A wombat leg. "Eat up!" he says.

Joey looks at you and yells, "Yeah, eat! Eat! Mmmm, the wombat is yummy in my tummy." You wonder how much cake is actually making it to his tummy. Most of it seems to be on his face.

[Turn to page 182.]

You decline the cake and force yourself to eat the so-called lunch that your mom packed for you. Justin Clocknee, renowned for his frequent lunchroom trades, swoops in with a handful of gummy bears. Without a word, the deal is done—Justin walks away with the cake. Liza gives you a couple of gummy bears as a consolation prize. You can't help but have immediate regrets. That was a truly enormous piece of cake and it looked really, really good.

By the end of the day, which includes three hours of gymnastics practice, you are famished. When you get home, everyone has just sat down to dinner. A full plate of spaghetti and peas awaits you on the table. You wolf down your meal as though there is no tomorrow. When your parents ask how your day was, you point to your sister, Annabelle, signaling that they should ask her first while you eat. Annabelle tells your parents that she didn't know some of the words on her spelling test so she just looked at Nazar's test since he "always knows how to spell right." She is neither ashamed nor apologetic. Your parents spend the rest of dinner struggling to address this situation and, in the meantime, you finish your meal.

[Go to the next page.]

Your aunt, your uncle, and Cousin Joey arrive to celebrate Joey's third birthday, even though it was a week ago. He is actually celebrating his third birthday for the fifth time, each party held at a different relative's house. *He must be very confused*, you think.

Since Joey has a strange love of wombats, his ice-cream cake is decorated with a giant frosting wombat. Before you know what's happening, your uncle hands you an enormous piece of cake. A wombat leg. "Eat up!" he says.

Joey looks at you and yells, "Yeah, eat! Eat! Mmmm, the wombat is yummy in my tummy." You wonder how much cake is actually making it to his tummy. Most of it seems to be on his face.

You eat the piece of cake. It's pretty good, though the chocolate cake Liza had offered you in the lunchroom looked better. You go to bed pleased with yourself for having resisted temptation. You figure there will be many other occasions when you will either yield to or resist temptation, and you can figure it out as you go along. And you are right.

[Go to the next page.]

In fact, the next day you find yourself faced with an even more difficult decision: whether to expose a classmate's science project as a sham. Over the past month, everyone in your class has been working hard on their projects. For yours, you took a Super Soaker water gun, cut off the top, replaced it with a Gatorade cap, and bored a small hole in the cap, turning the device into a "Balloon Vacuum" that kids can use to suck up pieces of water balloon that are usually scattered on playgrounds. You distributed water balloons at your local playground, watched the kids engage in balloon warfare, and, when the battle was over, let the same kids try out three Balloon Vacuums. The invention was a success: the playground was balloon-free by the end of the day and the kids actually had fun cleaning up. You are pretty proud of your science project.

[Go to the next page.]

Today is the big due date and, having seen other kids' final products, you are certain you'll win the purple ribbon for the best science project. But then you see something alarming. On the way to recess you glance into Mr. Haller's classroom and spot a perfect replica of the Brooklyn Bridge, along with an in-depth description on poster board of the physics behind bridges. How did you miss that one? The model clearly did not come from a box, but you just can't believe a sixth grader produced something with that kind of elegance and precision. As your classmates head to the courtyard, you slip into the classroom for a closer look and see that the project is Michael Rosenberg's. And that's when you remember that Michael's mom has a fascinating job . . . as a professional bridge designer. She came into your class last year to describe her work and to answer that question that kids so frequently ask: what's the point of learning all this math in school? You have to admit, her presentation was really interesting.

[Go to the next page.]

While his science project is definitely better than yours, there is no way that Michael had anything to do with building this bridge replica, except maybe carrying it into homeroom. And yet he's going to win the purple ribbon!

You notice that there's no one around at this particular moment. Of course you would never damage another student's science project, but it only seems fair to point out to Mr. Haller the evident truth that Michael's mom did his entire project. After all, it's important to be honest. A simple plan comes to mind. You could just write on a piece of paper, "Michael's mom did his whole project," then tape the paper to the back of the poster board and let Mr. Haller take it from there.

[If you do attach a note to the back of
"Michael's" science project, go to page 157.]
[If you walk away, go to page 166.]

You bug your mom for her credit card information. A bit annoyed, she gets off the phone, puts down the ladle in her left hand and the checkbook in her right, and actually runs to your computer. A minute later you are reading chapter 1 of *Another Book About Dragons and Stuff.* It is painfully uninteresting. About three pages into it, you decide to scroll to the end and read the "About the Author" blurb.

Sure enough, Belinda Schoen, "an attorney with her own small law firm," is married to "Bert Schoen, a school teacher." *Lawyers should not try to write books for kids*, you think. You slog through the first chapter.

The next day, Mr. Schoen visits your homeroom, which is odd. Wearing a somber expression, he pulls out a note card and reads from it.

[Go to the next page.]

"Kids," he says, "it has come to my attention that many of you were able to access *Another Book About Dragons and Stuff* at no cost. It has also come to my attention that three of you did, in fact, access said book at no cost, in violation of our implied contract. Raise voice now and look really angry." (Mr. Schoen actually reads those words directly from his note card, not realizing they are instructions to himself.) Then he reads the last line: "I hereby demand that the perpetrators reveal themselves."

Holy cow! This just got serious, and as you look around the room you can see a number of your classmates fidgeting uncomfortably. Brooke Nelson is turning red. As ridiculous as this situation is—Mr. Schoen assigning his wife's book and now reading from a tiny note card clutched in his huge hands—you realize that he's got a point. Maybe it's stealing and maybe it's not, but it's definitely not right.

As the questioning continues, with any perpetrators likely on their way to the principal's office, you sit back and relax, relieved that you made the right decision and aren't among the guilty. You've got a good head on your shoulders.

THE END

You open up the attachment. A minute later you are reading chapter 1 of *Another Book About Dragons and Stuff.* It is painfully uninteresting. About three pages into it, you decide to scroll to the end and read the "About the Author" blurb.

Sure enough, Belinda Schoen, "an attorney with her own small law firm," is married to "Bert Schoen, a school teacher." *Lawyers should not try to write books for kids*, you think. You slog through the first chapter, then forward the book to twelve of your friends via email and go to bed.

The next day, Mr. Schoen visits your homeroom, which is odd. Wearing a somber expression, he pulls out a note card and reads from it.

"Kids," he says, "it has come to my attention that many of you were able to access *Another Book About Dragons and Stuff* at no cost. It has also come to my attention that three of you did, in fact, access said book at no cost, in violation of our implied contract. Raise voice now and look really angry." (Mr. Schoen actually reads those words directly from his note card, not realizing they are instructions.) Then he reads the last line: "I hereby demand that the perpetrators reveal themselves."

[Go to the next page.]

Holy cow! You heard the word "perpetrators" on this morning's news; the newscaster was describing two nineteen-year-old boys who were caught setting fire to a warehouse . . . and they were heading to jail! Panicking, you imagine that you would not do well in jail; it seems unlikely that you would be allowed to wear your denim poof skirt and hot pink tank top there.

As these thoughts percolate in your brain, Mr. Schoen stands in front of the class, silently waiting for the culprits to come forward. After about thirty seconds, you can't take it any longer. You shout out, "I did it, but please let me keep my denim poof skirt and hot pink tank top!"

[Turn to page 184.]

Madagascar is pretty funny, even for the umpteenth time. The next week, at recess, you mention to Madison that you and Liza almost watched a movie called *The Shining*. Madison is probably the toughest girl in your grade. She looks at you like you're crazy. "Are you crazy?" she asks.

She tells you that her fourteen-year-old brother, Jayden, watched *The Shining* three months ago. Since then, he has slept with his light on, clinging to Mr. Bubbles, the stuffed octopus that he carried with him everywhere until he was seven.

Good thing Liza and I passed on that one, you think, as you return from recess.

[Go to the next page.]

As you make your way back to class, you pass four tables of exotic-looking food. You had forgotten: today is Intercultural Day, where you celebrate other cultures and try diverse foods. You survey the labels: samosas from India, dumplings from China, plantains from Cuba, and pierogi from Poland. Since kindergarten, you have never actually tried any of the unfamiliar foods. You always go straight for the food your parents have contributed—and then to the ever-present box of donut holes.

Should you stick with what you know, or try something from a different culture and risk gagging? Those plantains look pretty slimy . . . but maybe you don't know what you're missing.

[If you stick with the food you know,
turn to page 56.]
[If you take a small bite out of a plantain,
turn to page 187.]

The movie is actually pretty boring for the first fifteen minutes, but you and Liza are just curious enough to keep watching. A half an hour later, you are both absolutely terrified. Shaking, she pauses the movie. Every time the lights of a passing car cross the living room walls and ceiling, you pull the covers over your head.

You both agree that watching this movie was a terrible mistake, but you are stuck, because if you stop watching it now, your imaginations will run wild and you'll have terrible nightmares. You need to get to the reassuring conclusion, the happy part that you're sure must be at the end of this freaky movie. So you keep watching.

Another half an hour goes by. Liza presses "Stop." You are both crying now. Liza wakes up her parents. After they get over their initial displeasure, they turn on all the lights in the house and stay up with you. By 2:00 a.m., you are so exhausted that you can't keep your eyes open.

You sleep for two hours and then you wake up to a horrific nightmare—the ghost of your dad holding a bloody ax and moaning, "I told you. I told you. . . ."

THE END

Are you three years old? It's a bright red button that says, "Do not push"! What good could possibly come from pushing it? Did you think that confetti would fall from the ceiling and a man in a suit would emerge from the back of the closet to announce through a microphone that you have won an all-expenses-paid trip to the Bahamas? Nope. Did you hope that a secret compartment in the wall would open and reveal two tickets to the biggest concert of the summer, along with backstage passes? Wrong again. Is it possible that the button, even if pushed slowly, is basically an emergency switch that shuts off all power in the school? Bingo.

The second you push the button, the world around you goes pitch-black. You are right across from a kindergarten classroom and can hear half of those kids starting to cry while one screams gleefully, "I'm a bat! I'm a bat!"

[Go to the next page.]

Suddenly the custodian, Mr. Dubois, is hovering over you. The mystery of who pushed the red button is even easier to solve than the mystery of the missing erasers. You are in the principal's office in a heartbeat. In another heartbeat, police officers and firefighters are there with you. In another heartbeat, you're in a car with your dad, who is wearing a suit and an expression you have never seen before, which can't be good. He doesn't speak to you until you get out of the car, and then he looks you straight in the eyes and says, "What were you thinking?"

It's a good question, and you don't have an answer. You'll have lots of time to think of one, though, since you're grounded for a month.

THE END

You do not push the red button. Instead, you satisfy your curiosity by simply asking Janet Quinn, who can usually be counted on to find trouble when it has gone missing. She tells you that it's an emergency switch that shuts off all power in the school. The next day you confirm this with the custodian, Mr. Dubois. He mentions that a fourth grader, Frankie Thurber, pushed it about ten years ago and that he was not able to get the lights back on, so the rest of the school day was canceled.

As a result, there was a make-up day of school on what should have been the first day of summer. The kids were exceptionally angry at Frankie that last day of school, and his safety would have been in jeopardy had he not been expelled two months earlier for setting a roll of toilet paper on fire in the boys' bathroom.

You definitely made the right decision in this case, and you continue to make other good decisions throughout the year.

THE END

With things patched up with Davina, you try to keep your mind on your schoolwork, but all you can think about is John.

At the end of the day, you meet him at the bus stop. You're both grinning. The whole thing still feels a little weird and awkward, but in the few minutes before the buses arrive, the two of you manage to come up with a brilliant plan. This coming Friday is an early dismissal day, and John's older sister, Lydia, will be picking him up. There is an ice-cream shop next to the school. You, John, and Lydia will go together!

Now all you need to do is run the plan by your parents. . . .

[Go to the next page.]

You imagine the conversation with your parents—who have already forbidden dating in the sixth grade—going something like this:

You: "Mom and Dad, John McGrath and I would like to go for ice cream after school on Friday. His sister, Lydia, can bring us. She's seventeen."

Dad: "What? Where does he live? I will rip out his throat!"

Mom: "No daughter of mine will be going out with a boy in sixth grade. You have to choose between this boy and us!"

Annabelle (your little sister): "Can I play games on your phone?"

Mom and Dad (together): "No!"

You (crying): "But I think I love him."

Mom: "You're too young to know what love is!"

Dad: "Go to your room. You are grounded for two and a half years!"

[Go to the next page.]

Here's how the conversation actually goes:

You: "Mom and Dad, John McGrath and I would like to go for ice cream after school on Friday. His sister, Lydia, can bring us. She's seventeen."

Long, long pause. . . . Your parents exchange numerous glances.

Mom: "Okay, honey, we'll speak to John's parents and Lydia first. If it's okay with them, you can go, and we'll send you with some money."

Dad: "Have fun."

[Turn to page 162.]

At the end of the school day on a Friday, you poke your head into Ms. Martinez's office as she's shutting down her computer and putting on her coat. She is young and well liked by all of the kids, including the sixth-grade boys, who sometimes talk about how pretty she is. Whether it's her big smile or the fact that she is not much taller than you, Ms. Martinez immediately puts you at ease. She asks you how everything's going and peppers you with questions about horseback-riding camp. It is so nice to talk to her that you completely forget why you came to see her in the first place until she asks, "So, what's on your mind?"

[Go to the next page.]

You tell her everything. You name names. At first you feel a bit like you are tattling, but before long it just feels like you are doing the right thing. Ms. Martinez listens, nods, and takes notes. She gives you a cup of water. When you are done she asks a couple of questions, which you answer, and then she thanks you for coming to her. On your way out, she says, "There's a difference between teasing and bullying, and I'm glad you know the difference. Bullying is a serious issue." As you leave for the weekend, you see Ms. Martinez turn her computer back on.

[Turn to page 170.]

You grab a marker and scribble, "Michael's mom did his whole project" on a piece of paper, then you tape the note to the back of the poster board. Feeling slick and clever (and vindicated), you run back outside and enter a game of freeze tag.

[Turn to page 159.]

Two days later Mr. Haller asks you to stay behind while your classmates head off to recess. "Do you know vat a code breaker does?" he asks you. You shake your head, vaguely recalling that he had mentioned something at the beginning of the school year about working as a government code breaker. A code breaker, he explains, "deziphers encryption." Mr. Haller sees the blank look on your face, realizes that you are struggling to decipher what he just said, and restates: "a code breaker reads zeecret mezzages." Where is he going with this? Uh-oh, the science project note you wrote.

Your initial reaction is to feign ignorance, but it's no use; you've been caught. Mr. Haller is angry. He tells you that it's not your place to play teacher.

[Turn to page 180.]

You decide not to get involved. The situation goes from bad to worse for Vijay. Kim and her gang eventually become bored with merely insulting Vijay, so they start pushing books off of her desk in class, knocking them out of her hands when she is holding them, and even reaching into her book bag to grab her things and toss them around. They also pull her long, braided hair and run away. Vijay is miserable. Eventually the teachers get wind of the situation. You pass by Ms. Martinez's office one day and catch a glimpse of Vijay crying on the sofa just as the door is closing.

You feel terrible for Vijay, but you have an idea. Maybe she could use a friend. You'll start hanging out with her more. You ask your mom to call Vijay's mom to see if Vijay can hang out.

[Turn to page 177.]

The big day finally arrives, and you go with John and Lydia to Mad Madeline's Ice Cream Parlor. You're wearing your favorite pair of jeans and a light blue T-shirt. Your hair is all flat-ironed and smooth—your mom helped you that morning.

The moment you step through the door at Mad Madeline's, Lydia sees her friends and leaves you and John alone.

[Go to the next page.]

You listen as John begins describing the best way to remove dirt from a skateboard wheel. That topic runs its course about the same time that you finish your ice-cream cone, but then, astonishingly, he transitions to how best to remove dog poop from a sneaker. You nod politely. Hmm. It turns out that John is actually pretty dull.

At least he's really cute, you tell yourself. But it gets worse. A mischievous grin crosses his face, and suddenly his hand is on your knee! Whoa, back off! You are extremely uncomfortable. There are people everywhere, but he's not taking his hand away.

[Go to the next page.]

Then, from the next table over, you hear a voice call your name. "Can you give me a hand with this?" asks Matt Thurber, a fellow sixth grader widely rumored to have a crush on you. He is struggling with the zipper on his book bag. This is your opportunity to escape from John McGrath, who is shooting you a look that says, "Don't you dare." If you walk away from him now, in front of everyone, it could very well mean the end of your first-ever date and your whole relationship, which has only lasted three days so far. And imagine the gossip!

[If you assure Matt he can handle the zipper himself, turn to page 167.]

[If you leave the table to go help Matt, turn to page 168.]

It's not easy, but you just walk out of the classroom. Michael wins the purple ribbon later that day, and you feel as though a great injustice has been done. The next day, all students present their projects to the class. This is practice for later in the week, when the science projects will be displayed in the cafeteria for parents and students to see. Michael is called to the front of the class. You perk up, half-hoping that he'll crash and burn like a flimsy wooden bridge. But he doesn't. In fact, he is able to clearly explain vertical and horizontal forces and how they factor into different types of bridges: beam bridges, arc bridges, and suspension bridges.

His explanation is really interesting, and you ask him a couple of questions about the Brooklyn Bridge, which he answers without even looking at his poster board. Then, you can't help yourself: "Did you build that replica of the Brooklyn Bridge all by yourself?" you ask.

He replies, "No, my mom and I did it together. Some of the pieces were too small for me to attach. It took us all weekend, probably about fifteen hours."

Wow, maybe he does deserve the purple ribbon after all.

[Turn to page 102.]

You stay frozen, not accepting Matt's invitation to leave the table. The next three minutes are the most uncomfortable three minutes of your life so far. Finally, Lydia announces that it's time to leave.

The next week you find out that those three minutes of utter discomfort at Mad Madeline's Ice Cream Parlor are just the beginning. The four additional minutes you suffer through when you see John on Monday are equally uncomfortable, as are the two minutes on Tuesday and the five minutes on Wednesday.

After that, you and John drift apart. Though you only "hung out" for a week, the whole ordeal has a lingering effect on you for the rest of the year. Your short-lived relationship with John powers the gossip mill for weeks to come. Sixth grade is lousy.

THE END

You leap from the table and enthusiastically offer to help Matt with the zipper on his book bag. It unsticks easily; you've always been good at fixing book bags.

When you return to the table, John is staring at you with an angry expression. Sure enough, this incident marks the beginning of the end of your brief relationship with John McGrath. You are heartbroken at first. At least you picture yourself heartbroken, along the lines of what you've seen TV characters go through after breaking up. But the truth is, after a couple of days, you find it remarkably easy to move on.

[Turn to page 178.]

You head to your room. Would it be lying not to say something? The guilt eats at you over the weekend, but you forget about it for the most part while watching *Pitch Perfect*. You'll reconsider on Sunday, after Sage's birthday party. But by the time Sunday comes, the incident with Mr. Haller is a distant memory. You accompany your dad and sister, Annabelle, to Whole Foods while your mom stays home and pays bills.

Your dad sends the two of you on a mission to find fruit. You and Annabelle have very different views on how ripe a bunch of bananas should be before you buy them. As you make your case for choosing bananas with no hint of green, you glance over your shoulder and spot your dad talking to an older gentleman.

Yikes, it's Mr. Haller!

[Turn to page 172.]

You have no idea what happened over the weekend, but by Monday morning, school is completely different, and not just because the kindergarteners' artwork is now featured on the wall outside the main office. (Annabelle's drawing stands out, as she has sketched herself with the body of an ostrich—Mom and Dad might get a note about that one.) It's not that Kim Basta is suddenly best friends with Vijay; far from it. It's that Kim, as well as every other kid who was bullying Vijay on a regular basis, is noticeably afraid of Vijay. When Vijay passes these kids in the hall, they either stare straight ahead or keep their eyes on the ground.

You wonder why they are so frightened. If Vijay notices it, she doesn't seem to care. She seems perfectly happy to be ignored by the kids who, just a couple of days ago, were terribly mean to her. She brightens up a little bit more with each passing day and soon makes a few friends.

[Turn to page 176.]

Tears well up in your eyes. Your parents are strict and they will not be pleased. But you manage to tell your mom the whole story, including the part about having detention during recess. Her brow furrows, but she just tells you to go wash up for dinner in her normal, calm tone of voice.

By the time you emerge from the bathroom, your dad is home and sitting down at the dinner table with the rest of your family. You notice the peas on your plate and involuntarily make a face. Your dad tells you that you have to eat them. "Eating your peas builds character," he says, and then he breaks down in laughter. Your mom is trying to contain her laughter, but the smile on her face betrays her.

Your parents make you write an apology to Mr. Haller. It is surprisingly easy to write and, when you are done, they let you watch *Pitch Perfect*. Things just get better from that day on. The highlight comes three weeks later, when your parents get you the cutest Cockapoo puppy for your birthday. You name him Haller.

THE END

You slink to the vegetable section. You are wearing a green dress. Perhaps it will serve as camouflage? Sadly, it does not. Sensing your dad's disapproving gaze, you turn beet red. You can tell by his expression that Mr. Haller is telling all—your joke, your collapsing in laughter (alone), your loss of recess privileges, and his requirement that you tell your parents.

He leaves after a few minutes, shuffling toward the cheeses. When you return to your dad, he is hopping mad. He doesn't care about the detention as much as he cares about your failure to tell him and your mom. "The cover-up is always worse than the crime," he says. He tells you that he is extremely disappointed in you and says that he and your mom will discuss this further.

[Turn to page 174.]

If anything, your mom is angrier than your dad when she hears the news. She is clearly appalled that Mr. Haller had to report the story because you had chosen not to tell the truth yourself. It's late, so you go straight to bed, unsure of the impending consequences. You await your punishment the next morning, but it doesn't come.

[Go to the next page.]

Three weeks pass, and Annabelle's birthday arrives (only four days before yours). She asks for the same thing that she has requested for the past two years—a chainsaw. Weird little girl. She gets a box that looks about the size of a chainsaw. She opens it and you can't believe your eyes. A dream-come-true Cockapoo puppy jumps out and licks her on the nose. She laughs with delight. "I'm going to name him Chainsaw!" she screeches, and the name, painfully, sticks.

This is no dream; it's a nightmare-come-true. Dazed by the whole scene, you look at your parents. They are looking at Annabelle and Chainsaw, but you know that they know you are looking at them. And you know it's your own fault that you're not the one naming this adorable puppy. With a quiet groan, you realize that this moment is probably building character.

THE END

You are sure that Ms. Martinez had something to do with the dramatic reversal of Vijay's fortunes, but you can't fathom how so much has changed so quickly. There's no way one school counselor could have met with all of the mean kids over the weekend.

In the middle of the week you wear your large turquoise hoop earrings and, for the first time in a while, Kim Basta has something to say about them: "Are those hula hoops on your ears?" You are annoyed by the comment but, after seeing what Vijay has been through, it doesn't bother you for more than a couple of minutes.

You await the backlash that will surely come if Kim finds out that you were the one who spilled the beans, but it never happens. Exactly one week after you told Ms. Martinez everything, you pass her in the hall. She smiles and winks at you. You smile and wink back. The rest of the year goes great. You have survived the sixth grade!

THE END

Your mom tries to schedule a get-together with Vijay, but her mom says that Vijay has too much going on after school and doesn't have the time. This strikes you as odd since you happen to know that Vijay has flute lessons on Tuesdays and Thursdays but is free the rest of the week. Well, you tried.

[Turn to page 183.]

As the school year progresses, John McGrath "hangs out" with each of your friends, one at a time, and none of those relationships end well. In fact, one of them ends with the police somehow involved, though the details remain foggy.

Years later, you are sitting on the beach with your husband, gazing at the sunset painting the horizon in reds and oranges. As your kids run along to play in the water, you turn to your husband and ask for the thousandth time about that day at the ice-cream shop, but he still refuses to tell you whether the zipper on his book bag was actually broken. You sigh fondly, replaying those memories of sixth grade. . . .

THE END

Mr. Haller picks up your science project, the Balloon Vacuum. He asks you how you managed to bore such a perfect-sized hole in the Gatorade cap—small enough to maintain the vacuum mechanism but large enough to suck in a balloon. On the verge of tears, you explain to him that your dad used different drill bits and bored about four holes before he finally got it right. You couldn't use the drill, so you just watched. He asks you how you figured out how a vacuum works. You tell him that you read a bunch of articles about it. He asks where you found those articles. You tell him that they just appeared on the breakfast table one morning. You hadn't thought about it before, but your mom probably printed them out while you were in bed. He asks you how long it took you to make a hundred water balloons to bring to the playground for the purpose of testing the Balloon Vacuum. You tell him it took only about half an hour because your dad and sister helped out.

[Go to the next page.]

Mr. Haller has made his point. Though you try to smile and congratulate Michael when he wins the purple ribbon at the science fair, you keep thinking about your effort to sabotage his project. You feel terrible, and there's no Balloon Vacuum to help you pick up the pieces.

THE END

You eat the piece of cake, frosting wombat leg and all. You've had better cake. Your mom pushes a plate of spaghetti and peas in front of you. She doesn't have to say anything; your parents have always been okay with dessert before dinner, but the rule is that you have to eat your dinner . . . or else.

Every time you take a bite of the spaghetti on your plate, it appears to multiply, as if the food is defying you. By the end of dinner, you are so thoroughly stuffed that you feel like you might burst. You make your way to bed, but you have trouble sleeping. You try counting sheep, but their legs are chocolate wombat cake slices. You wake up the next morning with terrible stomach pains, have to miss a day of school, and discover that in sixth grade it's extremely difficult to catch up with your schoolwork once you've fallen behind.

THE END

Lexi Nexus knocks Vijay's books out of her hands one day and you help her pick them up. Kim's crew sees this—you might as well have painted a target on your back. Now they try to knock *your* books out of your hands.

Then one day Vijay does not come to school. She's not there the next day either. Or the next. Or the next. In fact, you never see her again.

You imagine yourself making a bold statement to Kim and the others about how they drove Vijay away, but you never actually do it. Instead, you find yourself guarding your books and wishing that sixth grade would just be over.

THE END

Mr. Schoen gives you a confused look, but then he thanks you for "confessing." Brooke Nelson and Dave Slavin confess next, and the three of you are off to the principal's office.

Principal Knivner asks you all to sit down. Then he poses a series of questions. Interestingly, he is neither angry nor intimidating when he asks them, despite his reputation as an enforcer. In a weird way, it's almost fun to be here having this confidential talk among your classmates. All three of you take the opportunity to mention how bad the book is and agree that it is strange that you are required to read a book by your teacher's wife. He dismisses you after five minutes. You pass Mr. Schoen on the way out as he enters Principal Knivner's office with a nervous expression.

You spend the rest of the day on pins and needles, wondering what to make of the situation in the principal's office and trying not to think about the possibility that the police could show up and handcuff you in the courtyard. But it turns out there are no further consequences at school. When you step onto the afternoon bus, you breathe a sigh of relief.

[Turn to page 186.]

185

You breathed your sigh of relief too soon. The second you arrive at home and see your mom, you know—Principal Knivner has called her. Because you told her about the online book last night, there's absolutely no way of weaseling out of this one. The first thing she says to you is, "Opening the free copy of that book was not the brightest idea, but the fact that you forwarded it to all of your friends makes you the ringleader." In a measured voice, she lectures you on "piracy" (the unauthorized use or reproduction of something someone else has created, not the practice of attacking and robbing ships at sea) and says, "What you did was dishonest, and it may even be stealing."

The word "stealing" cuts deeply, and you run to your room, half-crying and half-apologizing to no one in particular. You bury your head in your pillow, covering it in snot, and yell over and over, "I don't wanna be a pirate!"

Searching for someone to blame, you spot Trusty, the stuffed giraffe that was resting next to you when you opened the attachment. You throw her across the room, as if it were her fault for failing to speak up, advising you to choose wisely, like Jiminy Cricket would have. At least you won't make this mistake again.

THE END

You take a small bite of a plantain. It is delicious! You devour it and move on to the dumplings—they are surprisingly tasty, even though you're not a big fan of the texture. You like the samosas, too, but not the pierogi. Before you know it, the celebration comes to an end. You are pretty full after all of this sampling, but you feel hungry in a whole new way. You decide to investigate more foods you've never eaten so that you can continue this tasting adventure beyond Intercultural Day. You ask a number of friends what they brought in today and what other foods they like most, and you come up with a list of things you'd like to try, including sushi, chicken tikka masala, and melktert.

You give this list to your dad when you get home. From that point on, about once a week he brings home something from your list and you try it at dinner. Every bite of a new food is a surprise—usually a pleasant surprise.

[Go to the next page.]

By the time you are thirteen years old, you have developed a taste for a wide array of foods from all over the world. This refined palate serves you well when you explore South America after college, when you spend a summer teaching in Northern Africa two years later, and when you honeymoon in Europe.

THE END

Acknowledgments

My deepest gratitude to Catherine Milligan. Witty, astute, thorough, and patient, you are not just a fantastic editor, but also an invaluable sounding board (not to mention a serviceable Ping-Pong player).

Special thanks to the various family members and fifth and sixth graders who provided insightful comments along the way.

Kate, my sister, and John, my brother—you are hereby acknowledged! Booya!

About the Author

Dave McGrail lives in New York City with his long-suffering wife, Lauren, and his wonderful daughters, Macy (sixth grade) and Delilah (second grade). When he's not writing, Dave enjoys mummifying his kids (on Halloween only), forcing them to sing "Happy Birthday" to Abraham Lincoln every February 12th, and completely embarrassing them by dancing in the street.